a novelization by
BRET NELSON

based on the original screenplay by
EDWARD D. WOOD, JR

Encyclopocalypse Publications
www.encyclopocalypse.com

Contents

Litmus Test for Weirdos

By Dana Gould

Greetings my friends. You are all interested in *Plan 9 From Outer Space*, for that is what you and I will be reading about for the rest of this book. And as this book will prove, *Plan 9* is more than a movie, it's a way of life. A password. A secret handshake that signifies membership in very select group: smart folks with big hearts and evolved senses of humor. I'm speaking, of course, about weirdos.

I was a weird kid. While my friends, brothers and cousins were out at football or baseball practice, I was holed up in my bedroom with a stack of *Famous Monsters* magazines, *MAD* magazines and a shelf full of Aurora "Frightening Lightening" monster model kits. Saturday afternoons belonged not to hunting or fishing but to Creature Double Feature on Boston's channel 56. With that pop culture diet, it was impossible not to brush up against *Plan 9 From Outer Space*. I hadn't seen it yet, but I knew about it. I knew about Bela Lugosi, obviously. I knew about Vampira. I knew who Tor Johnson was, if not by his acting, by his Don Post mask. But I hadn't seen *Plan 9 From Outer Space* yet. That would have to wait until I had made the transition from weird kid to full-fledged adult weirdo.

Not every weird kid grows up to become an adult weirdo.

Most, in fact, peel off when they turn sixteen. I'm speaking only about dudes, of course. That's when a young man's energies shift from *MAD* magazine and Aurora model kits to cars, beers and girls (though not in that order). But there are always a few, we merry few, who never fully let go of what got us through those pre-pubescent years, when Saturday afternoons meant Creature Double Feature and little else.

I turned sixteen in 1980. That same year, Michael and Harry Medved's book, *The Golden Turkey Awards* was published. It was in *The Golden Turkey Awards* that *Plan 9 From Outer Space* was awarded the dubious honor, The Worst Film Of All Time. And so began its slow ascent to cinematic immortality.

I finally saw *Plan 9 From Outer Space* in 1985. I was twenty-one. I liked punk music, I dressed like Elvis Costello, I read *RAW* comics and made my living in sweaty, smoke-choked comedy clubs. My high school friends were still in college or pursuing respectable careers. Some were already dating the people they would marry. Not me. I was a weirdo. All my new friends were weirdos. I ran in strict weirdo circles. And everyone I knew loved *Plan 9 From Outer Space*. *Plan 9* was the movie for weirdos.

Plan 9 had a bit of everything I loved. It was a horror movie. It was also a science fiction movie. It was made in the fifties and, for all its production woes, was crisply photographed in glorious black and white. It looked like a *Twilight Zone* episode but of course, was gloriously Goddamned nuts. And that is why *Plan 9* is not, despite *The Golden Turkey Awards*, The Worst Film Of All Time.

For whatever its worth, the Medved's don't feel that way either. Never did. That honor was awarded via reader's poll. But in the documentary *The Plan 9 Companion*, film critic Bill Warren points out that the worst crime a film can commit is to be boring, and *Plan 9*, whatever it is, is never boring. That is what sets it apart from all the other, "so-bad-they're-good" movies, like *Rat Pfink-A-Boo-Boo*, *Robot Monster* or *The Swarm*. Yes, those movies are bad, but they're just bad. And they're inevitably boring. *Plan 9* has a new trick up its sleeve every five minutes. The stentorian sermon of the Hawaii-Five-Oh-surf-coiffed Criswell has barely left the screen before we're thrust into the world's worst cockpit set. You're still laughing at Duke Moore scratching his eye with the barrel of his own pistol when Tor Johnson tries to say, "medical examiner." And on it goes.

For my weirdo friends and I, *Plan 9* quickly became a litmus test for whether or not someone "got it." It wasn't the only one of course. There were several. The Ramones, Monty Python, *Late Night With David Letterman*, *SCTV*, Albert Brooks, the aforementioned Mr. Costello. You didn't have to like them all, but I can't remember being close friends with anyone who didn't like most of them.

Now of course, this was all a long time ago. My oldest daughter is now the same age I was when I first saw *Plan 9*. Time and adult responsibilities have sanded my edges, but deep down, I'm still the same person that sat on the floor of my friend's crappy apartment, eyes glued to that scratchy VHS tape.

It will surprise no one to learn that Halloween is a big holiday in the Gould house. We go hard in the decorations department, and my kids usually host a rather sizable sleepover. One year, after the last trick-or-treater had gone home and the Jack-O-Lanterns had been blown out, I sat down by myself to watch *Plan 9 From Outer Space*, now spotless on pristine DVD. At one point, my daughter and her friends came marching through the living room on their way to the kitchen. As I sat there cackling at some Ed Woodian gem, my daughter explained to her friends, "This is my dad's favorite movie. He's such a weirdo."

Clever girl.

Dana Gould
April, 2024

PLAN 9
FROM OUTER SPACE

UNSPEAKABLE HORRORS
FROM OUTER SPACE
PARALYZE THE LIVING AND
RESURRECT THE DEAD!

Prologue

A TOWN OF PEOPLE

Aviation Officer Howard Wilson hadn't stopped rocking the pedals or the stick of his Bell H-13 Sioux since he lifted off. Any other day, winds like these meant all flights from the Tonopah Test Range, including his helicopter, were grounded. But since this mission wasn't happening (officially), and his passenger wasn't there (officially), he told himself the wind wasn't officially blowing, either.

Everything about this assignment felt unreal. Even today's date looked peculiar - February 29th, 1956.

Over the last 48 hours, he'd shuttled a lot of high-ranking military personnel and a few rocket-program civilians to the site of "The Breverton Incident." His current passenger, carrying no identification and introduced as "Colonel," stood out. He stood out by not speaking.

The others never stopped talking. They had a lot of questions about the incident and the attackers. Wilson understood. They wanted to settle their nerves and break the quiet on the eighty-mile run over the empty Nevada desert. But his orders said to keep secrets and fly low.

"Don't know anything about it," he'd tell them. "In fact, this is my first flight out there." Repeat passengers got the same line.

But the colonel had no questions. No chatter at all. And nothing shook him on this rough ride. The bubble cabin of the Sioux rocked like they were traveling by covered wagon. Yet, this man leaned into the pitches and took the bumps without comment. Three times he had to use the overhead grab bar to keep on his side of the chopper, but he never said a thing. And one hand always stayed near his attaché case.

A gust pushed the chopper ten feet sideways, and the colonel bounced hard. Again. This man had rank. Wilson felt he had to say something.

"Sorry, Sir."

The colonel pressed the cans on his headset tight to his ears and spoke into his mic. "Repeat, please," he said.

"Apologizing for that last pitch, Sir," said Wilson. "These gusts come fast. Sometimes I can't counter."

The colonel scanned the mesas surrounding them. "Son, when I was your age, they had me bucking all over the cargo hold of a C-47, then they made me jump out. This is a luxury seat. You don't need to fret about my comfort. Just fret about keeping this whirlybird on course."

"Sir, yes Sir," said Wilson.

"How much further to the site?" asked the colonel.

"I haven't made this run before. But if the coordinates are accurate and there isn't too much sand blowing around, we should have visual once we're over the next rise."

Wilson drew the helicopter east until they were running parallel with Gypsum Highway, the only road in a hundred-mile radius. The winds moved swaths of sand on and off long stretches of the asphalt, making sections of the highway fade away then return. But he didn't need to follow that black line to keep his bearings. The site lay straight ahead to the northeast.

"There," said Wilson. "Your two-o-clock, Sir."

The highway terminated at a small town called Breverton, built to house the workers at a newly-opened gypsum mine. A place so new it wouldn't be on the maps until next year. The population had just grown to 432 people.

Until a few days ago.

Now, the wind pushed a vast column of smoke west across the desert. It rose from the remains of Breverton.

"There's two little hillocks to the side of the road, a few miles before the town," said Wilson. "Between them, they've put up some Quonset huts. Lots of gear. Lots of trucks. That's the LZ."

On the second attempt, Wilson landed the Sioux right on the mark. Major David Carlson stood waiting for them. He escorted both Wilson and the colonel off the makeshift landing pad. "I wish I had something to offer you, Colonel, but water and instant soup is all we've got right now."

"Water sounds fine, Major Carlson," said the colonel.

Wilson hadn't seen any kind of introduction. These men knew each other.

"That hut over there, you'll find water to drink and wash up with," said Carlson. "You go ahead, I'll be there in a minute."

"Right," said the colonel. He turned to Wilson. "Thanks for getting me here in one piece." The two of them passed a salute back and forth, then the colonel disappeared into the Quonset hut.

Carlson leaned into Wilson and spoke in his ear. "I can't believe they're allowing flights with these winds. We're going to lose more men."

"There's nothing logged, Sir," said Wilson. "There isn't a flight, so how can there be danger?"

The major felt his frustration rise, then he swallowed it. Over these last few days, he'd eaten triple portions of frustration and double talk.

This entire operation was off the books. Nothing on paper unless absolutely necessary. If something had to be written, they used a "flash folder," specially treated paper and files that burned in seconds and left no ashes. They were kept in large envelopes with a pull-string along the side. One tug and the whole thing ignited.

The major sent Wilson to check out his helicopter, to get it ready for the return flight. Then he pulled himself together. He had to make his report.

Inside the structure, he found the colonel seated at the rough table. His face dripped wet. "There aren't any towels," he said. Both men shared a laugh.

"Out here, you'll be dry in a minute," said Carlson, "It's good to see you, Colonel Edwards. I wish it wasn't under these circumstances, though."

"Is it worse than Virginia?" asked Edwards. He spun the numbered dials on his attaché case and pulled out a notebook.

"Much worse."

"Okay, let's have it."

"This started seventy-two hours ago," said Major Carlson. "A squadron of Lockheed Starfighters on patrol engaged a saucer, about three hundred miles to the south. The saucer sped north, and the fighters pursued." Edwards nodded, moving his pen quickly. He filled the page with a series of swirls and slashes; a code known to six people.

Carlson pointed at the ceiling. "Right here, just above us, this is where they caught up with the saucer. Then the fighters let loose with that new ordinance."

"The splinter rounds? Did they have any effect?"

"Must have, because the saucer fired back."

The information hung in the room for a moment. Colonel Edwards scribbled a few more coded lines, then spoke. "That's a first," he said.

"Yes," said Carlson. "Over the radio, one of the pilots called it a 'beam weapon.' Said the saucer emitted an energy ray, then turned and tilted, using the beam like a mile-long cutting tool. It went right through the jets. There's wreckage in building three. You'll see, it's like they were sliced with a precision torch. Wiped them out in minutes."

"And the town?"

"The damn beam moved through everything," said Carlson. "There are deep grooves charred into the desert floor. It vaporized any building it crossed and most of the neighboring structures as well. Outside the strike point, intense heat and fire. The mine got hit, too. The whole thing melted into the landscape. Then the saucer flew off like nothing happened."

Carlson crossed the room to the water jug. He poured himself a cup and drained it, then peered out the dusty window. "No one stood a chance, in or out of the mine," he said. "There's nothing left and it's all still burning. We haven't found a way to put it out." Edwards joined him.

He saw nothing but smoke along the horizon. "With our standard rounds and rockets," he said, "I don't think we caused any damage to the saucers, but we did hold them back. We convinced them to flee. This new ordinance, these splinter rounds. Sounds like we've poked the bear."

"What will you do?" asked Carlson.

"You know how it is, Dave. I'm in charge of Field Activities, of implementation. The planning, the decisions, those are coming out of the Pentagon and Vandenberg. All I can do is log my reports and recommendations and hope my next round of orders make sense."

"And it's all off the books," said Carlson. "Hell, everybody thinks Vandenberg is still a driving school for tanks. Nobody knows about the rocket program there." He went to the door and called to a soldier he had waiting outside. The soldier gave him a metal case the size of a cigar box.

He dismissed the soldier and secured the door, then closed the blinds on the windows. He opened the case and handed it to Edwards. "Here's a little leverage for your next report," said Carlson.

Inside the case, three plastic tubes rested in three foam-rubber slots. Each tube contained a single metallic fragment. The largest piece was the size of a dime.

"Are these what I think they are?" asked Edwards.

"Came off the saucer," said Carlson. "My report recommends not using splinter rounds or any other new ordinance until the eggheads at Vandenburg have done the metallurgy on those bits. Until they've found a weakness, a *real* weakness."

"I'm with you," said the colonel. "We lost jets, pilots, and a town full of people. The saucer lost these shavings."

Two days later, the fires were out. A few newspapers carried a story about an explosion in Breverton, caused by the rupture of a natural gas pocket during mining operations. A small story. And the town never did appear on a map.

ONE

Future Events Such as These

Last year at the Fourth of July cookout, Jeff Trent paid close attention to his uncle, a master of the charcoal kettle. Now that he had a patio and grill of his own, Jeff cooked outdoors every chance he got. Coals and lighter fluid ("liquid Boy Scout" his uncle called it) were always on hand.

Chicken burned easily over the brickettes, but Jeff's uncle showed him how to manage it. "You gotta keep the pieces moving," he said. "Never stop running away from the flareups. It takes half an hour to do it right. And you gotta watch it the whole time."

And now, early on this Tuesday afternoon, Jeff's bird looked every bit as good as his uncle's. With five minutes to go, all the pieces were safely finishing on the coolest part of the grill.

He heard the news on TV. Jeff looked through the screen door to the television set in the den. A man in a black tuxedo spoke to the camera. His wavy hair held a tight spit curl in front.

"Greetings, my friends," said the well-groomed man. "We are all interested in the future, for that is where you and I are going to spend the rest of our lives. And remember my friends, future events such as these will affect you in the future."

It wasn't the news. It was that psychic on Channel 13. "You're watching this guy again?" called Jeff.

"Yeah," answered Paula Trent. She chopped tomatoes on a cutting board in the kitchen, next to the den. "I saw him on Jack Paar yesterday. Said invisible insects are going to swarm Indiana. They're going to bite everyone and dig under their skin. Isn't it wild?"

"Well, I'd better call my brother and tell him to get some bug spray."

The man on the TV leaned toward the camera. "You are interested in the unknown, the mysterious, the unexplainable. That is why you are here."

Paula turned slowly, speaking in a low voice and wiggling spooky fingers at her husband through the kitchen window. "Mysterious! Unexplainable! Your future is in the future!"

"Food is in your future!" he said, waving a drumstick at her with a pair of tongs. "This chicken is ready, just needs to sit for a few minutes." He brought the plate full of poultry into the kitchen and draped a piece of foil over it.

"Smells so good," she said. "The salad is in the ice box, all set. We need a name for this. It's late for lunch and early for dinner."

"Sorry Darling, it's the only time I've got," said Jeff, washing his hands in the kitchen sink. "This red-eye route is the best I can get for now."

"I'm not complaining, Flyboy. At least it's a turnaround tonight, right?"

"Yes. We land in Chicago then come right back, no layover. Should be home just before sunrise."

They kissed, and a siren interrupted them. A motorcycle cop led a line of cars down their street.

Paula rested her head against Jeff's chest as she watched the cars go by their patio. "I sent some flowers to the office," she said. "Hope the old man is all right."

Jeff and Paula Trent got married two years ago. They moved into this bungalow in the city of San Fernando, California back in

November. They got a steep discount against the asking price because the property bordered the Briar Glade Cemetery. Tombstones stood just over the patio fence.

They ignored the friends and family who told them not to pull the trigger on the purchase. It was so much house for the money, so much closer to Burbank Airport than their old apartment in Alhambra. Jeff flew for American Airlines, so that proximity meant a lot.

And it was quiet, except for the sirens when a funeral procession rolled by. The service today was for the lady who sold them the place.

"Never thought she'd be the one to go first," said Paula. "Her husband's got what, fifteen or twenty years on her?"

"Eighteen years his junior, according to your mother," said Jeff. "She'd know, too."

"What do you mean?" asked Paula. "You calling my mother nosey?"

"No, not at all," he said, quickly. "She lived out here when those two first got together. When we told her we were working with North Valley Realty, she mentioned it."

"Oh yeah. Quite a scandal, she said. Everyone called him a dirty old man, and her a gold digger."

"Yes, that's what your mother said. And you said it too, just now, but I still feel like I might be in trouble."

"Oh, you're in trouble all right, mister." Paula pulled him close.

"Can I make it up to you? Free chicken dinner? It's ready."

Paula held him tighter. "Bet it'll be delicious cold. Come on, let's get you packed."

"I'm already packed," said Jeff.

"I don't think so," she said, tugging him toward the hallway. "Come with me, Flyboy. I need to make sure your gear is stowed properly."

✴ ✴ ✴

Two men with shovels stood at a respectful distance from the mourners at the graveside. Both felt the clock working against them. Hugh Thomas and Jason Reynolds, the gravediggers, had other tasks to do this afternoon, but they were stuck here until this service ended.

"Don't know if we can get the other hole dug," whispered Jason. "Soil over there in Lot Fourteen is too soft. We'll have to shore it up as we go."

"It'll be a slog all right," said Hugh.

"These folks have a while to go yet. By the time we get this hole filled in and tamped down, we'll already be losing the sun."

"You're right," said Hugh. "It'll be dark soon. We'll have to find a bar."

At the graveside, the pastor droned on, glancing at his Bible more out of habit than necessity. "To everything there is a season, a time to every purpose under the heavens. A time to be born, a time to die ..."

The old man standing next to the pastor wasn't paying him any mind. He focused on the casket, resting below. They had just finished lowering it into the grave where it would stay forever. Most of the roses were still on top.

She hadn't been home in three weeks. Emergency room all the first night, then to Valley General, to the bed she died in. And now, here he was, putting her in the ground at Briar Glade.

His family had a small vault here, but she wanted nothing to do with it. They talked about it a few years back. "It's creepy," she said, "like a crypt from an old movie." So, she got herself a deal on a plot by some trees. "Get a simple marker and I'll be fine. Can we stop talking about it now? Let's just hope I won't be needing it anytime soon."

And here he was, putting her in the ground at Briar Glade. Too soon. She wasn't supposed to go first. He was so much older. She had so much more to do.

"... a time to plant, and a time to pluck up that which is planted ..."

The old man's gaze drifted from the casket to a pair of rough looking men. They stood by the trees, leaning on their shovels.

"Crap," whispered Hugh, "That old man is looking over here." He pulled off his weathered straw hat and held it in both hands as he looked down.

"I can't tell where he's looking," said Jason, squinting toward the service. "My eyes must be going."

"You're out in the sun all day. I keep telling you to wear a bigger hat."

"Oh, be quiet Mother," said Jason. He removed his striped touring cap and bowed his head.

"Can we just go to the bar now and fill this hole tomorrow?" Hugh whispered.

Jason stifled a laugh. "Shut up, dammit. Show some respect."

The old man saw that the gravediggers, like him, weren't paying any attention to the pastor. Those two were the only people here who weren't lying. They just wanted to get their work done and leave. It's what the old man wanted, as well.

Decades ago, he opened the first real estate office operating at this end of the Valley. She was a young agent working for him. As she signed more clients, he scheduled more meetings with her. Meetings became lunches. Lunches became dinners. And these lunches and dinners became less about property sales and more about falling in love.

Everyone had it wrong about his feelings for her. Their feelings for each other. Twenty years back and right up to today, wrong.

All the time, he heard them whispering at restaurants, the movies, and especially at church. He got used to ignoring them long ago. Now, every one of those gossips and busybodies couldn't wait to give their condolences.

A card from the Five and Dime: *Sincerest thoughts in your moment of grief.*

A note on a casserole, left on his porch: *Hope this brings you some comfort. It freezes really well.*

Spoken by the produce manager at the grocery: *Always liked her, such a shame, so young*.

Liars. All of them. They couldn't wait for his marriage to fall apart. They got so jealous when it didn't, and their own sham relationships went to pieces. Judging, mocking all the time.

The only people being honest today at Briar Glade were those men with the shovels. They just wanted to get on with it.

The old man felt a hand on his arm. "Excuse me," said the pastor, "we're moving to the chapel now."

The pastor led the group away, and the men with the shovels trotted to the grave and started filling it in. "We don't gotta dig that other hole today," said Hugh. "Funeral Director ain't checking on it until tomorrow afternoon. The burial don't happen until the day after."

"Well then, as long as there's a grave dug at Lot Fourteen before lunch tomorrow, we're fine," said Jason.

"Right. After this we'll get to the shed, plug the cart into the charger, and make sure we've got everything loaded. All sorted-like. Start in tomorrow morning at 5:30."

"Let's make it 6:30. More light then," said Jason.

"All right, 6:30. We'll take the cart to Lot Fourteen and have the whole thing dug before lunch."

"You," said Jason, "are a genius. With every shovel of this here dirt, I can feel my beer getting closer."

TWO

That's Nothing from This World

Edith Packer couldn't see the sun yet; it was still rising behind the plane. Soon the light would creep in around the window shades.

As she locked away the coffee mugs, she wondered if she'd ever get used to the smell of these red-eye flights. Every one of the forty suits flying from Chicago to Burbank sat crooked, passed out. Sweating booze and a bad meal. Each row had a drooler. Each row had a snorer. In some cases, they were the same person.

The plane had passed Arizona, and in less than an hour she'd have to wake them all to prepare for landing.

She remembered the want ad from American Airlines, promising good pay and flexible hours. So long ago.

The pay was fine. They gave her a raise at the start of her fourth year. But the hours were still about as flexible as a tire iron. At least she got to travel.

The younger girls got assigned to the daytime flights. Still, that nice Mr. Shafner had a ticket for this overnight run at least twice a month. He liked to take Edith on the town. She'd see him next Wednesday.

Up in the cockpit of the Douglas DC-7, Jeff Trent and his co-pilot Danny Sherman saw the sunrise behind them reflecting off everything in their view. Nearly time to start the real work. Nearly time for their descent.

Jeff had a firm grip on the controls. Danny checked the instrument panel and made notes in the flight log. "Quarter to six," said Danny. "Yup, right on schedule. I can almost see the San Fernando Valley, way out there."

"You better radio in for landing instructions," said Jeff.

"Right." Danny snugged up his headphones, brought the handset to his chin, and locked the *talk* button. "Burbank Tower, this is American Flight 812, over."

All they heard was static. "Wouldn't surprise me any if he's asleep this time of the morning," said Danny.

A voice crackled in their headphones. "American Flight 812, this is Burbank Tower. If I were asleep, you'd never get on the ground. You'd be up there for good. Over."

The voice belonged to Mac Robbins, an air traffic controller at Burbank. Hearing him brought smiles to the cockpit. It meant they'd be home soon.

"Danny, if you're gonna crack wise you have to let go of the button," said Jeff.

Danny made a production out of unlocking the handset, then he pressed *talk*. "You got me that time, Mac," he said. "Let's try again. This is American Flight 812. We are requesting -"

The plane lurched hard. Danny's elbow slammed into his armrest, and he dropped the handset. Both he and Jeff felt their seatbelts strain against the motion as a fierce radiance poured through the windshield, forcing the men to turn their heads.

Then their aircraft settled. The light subsided revealing a flying saucer hovering in front of the plane.

"Holy mackerel," said Danny.

Jeff checked the instruments. They were still headed to Burbank at the proper velocity and altitude. "Whatever it is," he said, "it's matching our course and speed."

They'd left Mac Robbins hanging. His voice came over their headphones again. "American Flight 812, say again please. You cut out. Over." Danny fumbled for the handset; his eyes locked on the saucer.

Back in the cabin, a few passengers woke up when the plane rocked. Edith reassured them. "Just turbulence," she whispered. "I'll go check in with the pilots, but I'm sure everything is fine."

Edith knew this wasn't turbulence. She moved through a tiny hall, a door, and a set of curtains to reach the flight deck, where the light hurt her eyes.

"Is there any trouble?" she asked.

"Look for yourself," said Danny.

Once her eyes got used to the glare, Edith saw the saucer. Although the alien craft was disc shaped, from this angle she only saw its edges. To her, it looked like a giant, glowing cigar. "What in the world?" she said.

Danny shook his head. "That's nothing from this world."

The headphones buzzed with Mac's voice again. "Burbank Tower to American Flight 812, are you all right? Please respond. Over." Danny became aware of the handset.

He pressed *talk* just long enough to say, "Stand by Burbank Tower. Over."

"Edie," said Jeff, "do you suppose the passengers saw it?"

"I doubt it. Most of them are asleep," she said. "Besides, they don't have any way to see out in front of the plane. Some of them felt the jolt, though."

"I think it's breaking off," said Danny.

The saucer moved away, slowly in a straight line ahead of them. Then, with a flash, it zipped vertically, out of sight. California at dawn filled their view, as if the strange vessel never existed.

Jeff checked his instruments. Course and speed were unchanged. They were still on time. "Edie," he said, "get the passengers ready for landing, all right? Let's keep it quiet until we get instructions."

"Right," said Edie. "But we need to talk to somebody about this."

"Count on it," said Jeff.

Edith Packer returned to the cabin. Jeff turned to Danny and took a deep breath. "Okay, let's call it in."

"I'll call," said Danny, "but I don't know what I'm gonna call it." He pressed the *talk* button. "American Flight 812 to Burbank Tower, sorry to keep you waiting, Mac. We are requesting landing instructions. And we have something to report."

Unseen by anyone on American Flight 812, the saucer continued on its course toward the northmost section of the San Fernando Valley. It landed quietly behind a deep knoll at the Briar Glade Cemetery.

* * *

At 6:53, the cart carrying Jason, Hugh, and their gear arrived at Lot Fourteen. The rising sun provided just enough gray light for them to start their work.

"Is there any coffee left?" asked Jason, rubbing his temple. Hugh rummaged around the cart and came up holding a plaid-patterned cylinder with a plastic cup on top. He shook it, but it made no sound.

"Empty, friend," said Hugh. "I told you not to have that last boiler maker."

"Yes, you did, and I'm paying for it hard enough without the 'I told you so' on top. Let's do the template."

The men laid out the boundaries of the grave using two-by-fours, a carpenter square, stakes, and twine. Hugh probed the ground with a spade.

"Pretty soft," he said. "We should still use the picks to start it, though."

Jason was already breathing hard, and the hard work hadn't begun. "After we dig this out, I may want to climb in," he said. "Cover me and say a few words, okay?"

"You do look pale," said Hugh. "There ain't no coffee, but there's jug on the cart with water. Throw some on your face."

Nodding, Jason stepped slowly toward the cart. A strange sound stopped him. A whirring tone. When he turned his head, it pitched lower. He moved back the way he came, and the sound pitched higher.

Hugh caught the same noise. "Do you hear anything?" he said.

"Thought it was just my head swimming," said Jason. "Is it some kind of swarm?"

"Never heard bugs sound like that. It goes higher and lower, don't it?"

"I thought it did," said Jason.

The two men walked slow circles, trying to determine the sound's origin. The tone shifted with each of their turns, and their unease grew. "It's coming from everywhere," said Hugh.

"Don't like hearing noises," said Jason, "especially when there ain't supposed to be any."

"Yeah," said Hugh. "Sort of spooky-like."

And in the next instant, the sound stopped. All sounds stopped, even the birds. For a minute, the men waited.

Jason broke the silence. "Maybe we're getting old."

That got a smile out of Hugh. "Maybe. Well, whatever it was, it's gone now."

It started again, louder than before.

"Best thing for us too," said Jason. "Gone!"

They ran the twelve strides to the cart, surrounded in darkness.

"How did it get so dark all of the sudden?" asked Hugh. "Weren't a cloud in the sky. It feels like it's nighttime."

"Now who's been drinking?" said Jason. "You can't be in day one second and night the next."

The nearby brush moved. Twigs snapped and leaves rustled. The men got closer together. "Maybe it's a big raccoon," said Hugh.

"I don't want to find out," said Jason. They piled into the cart and his hand fumbled next to his ankles, trying to find the lever to turn it on.

The brush parted and a figure emerged, a woman. She moved through the shadows toward them, and the curious whirring sound intensified.

"Now who is this?" asked Hugh.

"Don't want to find that out either," said Jason.

"Then get the cart started!"

"The lever's not doing nothing. It ain't got juice!"

The woman was only a few yards away now, close enough for the men to see her impossibly pale skin. Her gaunt frame. "It's the lady, the one they put down yesterday," said Jason.

"Run!" said Hugh. The men leapt from the cart and sprinted down the path. Ahead of them, somehow, the gaunt woman waited with her claw-like fingers reaching.

They spun around and ran the opposite way. And again, she waited in front of them. This time, her slender fingers tore into them. Hugh and Jason collapsed, screaming in the early morning sun. She fell on top of them and continued her relentless slashing long after their shrieking stopped.

* * *

The old man managed some intermittent sleep through the night, peppered with fragmentary dreams. Now, the morning light shone around the blinds.

He gave up on sleep and got himself dressed.

There was a small gathering at his sister-in-law's house after the funeral yesterday. The old man didn't stay long. His wife said she didn't want a "celebration." She wanted everyone to take that time and spend it with someone they loved, because there will come a day when they wished they had more time.

Even one more minute.

He went outside to get the *Times*, but the damn paperboy

missed the driveway again. The old man found it in the flower bed.

The newspaper sat among the roses she planted in the summer. A hot day, but she was determined to get all four of those little bushes in. Afterward, her cheeks were flushed from the sun. He told her they were the same shade as the roses.

This morning, her cheeks, her face was all he saw when he looked into the flower bed.

He saw her everywhere. Every bit of this house manifested something about her. Something she bought recently. Something she used each day. How could he live here?

There were practical concerns as well. What would he do with all the things on her side of the closet? Around her sink? What of the secret things in her nightstand drawer?

Any other day, he'd go to the office and get lost in work. Make the rest of existence disappear in the periphery. But there would be people there with concerned expressions painted on their faces. They'd come at him, slowly shaking their heads.

I only just heard, how are you holding up?

A fantastic woman. I'm lucky to have known her.

Why are you even here? You shouldn't be working, go be with family.

Liars. Gossips looking for news to spread. Minutes later, they'd be whispering down the phone.

I heard she was more a nurse than a wife.

He looked like hell. Is he drinking again?

You didn't hear it from me, but she had the diagnosis for weeks before she said anything. Didn't want him to worry.

All lies. They shared everything. Made every decision together. Right down to the last big dose of morphine that ended her pain. She went out with her head on his chest, sleeping. It's what she wanted, what they decided.

And like everything else in their life together, it was nobody's damn business.

At lunchtime, he put on a suit and a cloak and drove the Chrysler out to Malibu, top down all the way. She loved it there. He went to The Sea Lion and ordered a plate of abalone, her favorite.

Looking through the restaurant's vast, ocean-facing window, he peered at the water and tried to remember everything about her. Remember her joyous living. She said it was what she wanted, for him to remember the happiness of the last twenty years. Not the agony of these last few weeks.

So here, by the waves, he tried to remember joy.

Once he finished his meal, he paid the check and dropped a ten-dollar-bill on the table for the waitress. Then, he left The Sea Lion and walked across Pacific Coast Highway against the traffic signal. A Mercedes 170V struck him and he died at the scene from internal injuries.

Was he oblivious to the signal, lost in the agony of his grief? Or was this how he made the agony end?

That was nobody's damn business.

THREE

Getting Dark

The pastor's voice echoed in the vault at Briar Glade. A week ago, the same people had come together for his wife's service. Now they gathered again for the old man's interment.

His family's vault was in the oldest part of the cemetery. The carved doors hadn't been opened for 32 years. After the service, they'd likely never be opened again. He was the last of the line.

The pastor spoke the end of the passage, "I know that there is nothing better for people than to be happy and to do good while they live," he said, glancing now and again at his Bible. "That each of them may eat and drink and find satisfaction in all their toil. This is the gift of God."

He closed his bible and led the mourners out of the vault. The pastor invited them to come to the chapel if they wished. Bernard and Shirley Klemens decided to forego it.

Bernard was assistant manager North Valley Realty. He and Shirley were among the few who counted themselves as friends of the old man and his wife. They shared dinners, day trips, and thousands of hands of exceptionally competitive pinochle.

Ever since the old man brought his wife to the hospital, Bernard had been running most of the business. That position just became permanent. He wished one of them was still here to lean on. He didn't know if the office could survive with both of them gone.

He'd think about it later. "C'mon honey," he said. "Let's go get some chianti and a plate of linguini at Emilio's. They loved the place."

Shirley stared across the grounds. "It still seems like it's not real, you know? First his wife. Then he ... well, you know what they say he did."

"Doesn't matter what *they say*," said Bernard. "We don't know what he did, and neither does anybody else. He might have been lost in his thoughts, or the driver that hit him lied about what happened. All we do know is, it's tragic." He lit a cigarette then put his hand on her shoulder. "It's getting late, let's be on our way."

"Yeah," she said. "Chianti sounds nice."

They walked the path, meandering toward the far-off parking area. It looked as if no one had set foot in this part of the cemetery for ages.

"Where was her service, anyway?" he asked. "I'm all turned around."

"Over the hill there, next to those high trees," she said. "I wonder why they aren't together."

"They might be," said Bernard, looking skyward. "Who's to say?"

She giggled and smacked his shoulder. "You know what I mean. She's in the ground over by those trees and he's back there in the, um, crypt? Tomb? Whatever you call it."

"The pastor called it a vault. Maybe it's a family tradition? A superstition of some sort? Maybe he snores, so she wanted her own place."

"You are awful." She smacked him again and he ran a few steps ahead of her.

"And you are the prettiest girl here," he called.

"Prettiest girl in the graveyard," she said. "Thanks a lot."

He let her catch up, and when she did, he gave her a peck on the cheek and tossed away the remains of his cigarette.

"Bernie!" she said. "Are you for real?"

"What?" he'd upset her but didn't know how.

"Show a little respect." She took a few steps off the path. "This is hallowed ground and you're tossing your butts like it's the racetrack or something." Shirley reached between two headstones and snatched the offending stub.

Her husband tried to extract himself from the doghouse. "I'm sorry, Honey … at least let me get it, you're in those heels."

"I already got it, Galahad. Thanks anyway." When she stood up, something past the headstones caught her eye. Something with stripes.

She leaned in for a better look. It was a hat.

Laying on top of a corpse.

Resting next to another corpse.

And even in the poor light, she saw the blood stains on their ripped flesh and clothes.

She screamed, covered her eyes with her hands, and screamed again.

* * *

The San Fernando Police Department served a quiet city. Their headquarters stood at the end of a quiet street. The quiet drove Lieutenant Jonathon Harper nuts.

Five years ago, Harper transferred from Philadelphia, where he was on City Watch. He and his wife were looking for someplace less frantic. Well, she was, anyway.

At first, he couldn't find his place in this rural assignment. But as time passed, he came to appreciate the community. He liked the people he served. He liked the department, especially the commander, Inspector Daniel Clay.

Clay had thirty years on the force. His large family owned big stretches of farmland in his native Sweden and out in Simi Valley going back over a hundred years. His parents came to America when Clay was in his teens, and he fell in love with the cop shows on the radio. Once he graduated high school, he went straight into the police academy and graduated top of his class. He traded tractors for patrol cars.

The San Fernando PD had less than 50 officers, and Clay knew each of them personally. Not afraid to get his hands dirty, either. He and Harper got along just fine.

But the quiet out here made Harper nervous. When he worked in the big city, quiet meant danger. It meant trouble lurked, ready to come at you.

So far, the whole afternoon had been absolutely still, putting the Lieutenant on edge. He sat with Inspector Clay in the main conference room going over the timesheets they'd be sending along to County the next day.

T's to cross, I's to dot, and column after column of hours and names to check and double check. Both men jumped when Officer Paul Kelton erupted into the room. He started speaking before he got through the doorway.

"Jaime was just on the radio," he said, pointing down the hall in the direction of the radio. "He's asking for backup. The coroner and everything. Him and Larry are on that call at Briar Glade. He says it's just gruesome."

Harper narrowed his eyes at the rookie. "I think you meant to say *Officer Greene* and *Officer Tucker* have asked for backup, right?"

"Um, yes, them. Sorry Lieutenant." Paul Kelton had just one year out of the academy. He had a lot to prove. Often, his actions came a couple of steps ahead of his thoughts.

"Hold on a minute," said Clay, his gruff Swedish accent tenderizing the words. "Where was this call?"

"Briar Glade Cemetery, Sir. Came in about an hour ago. Caller said they found some dead bodies." Kelton kept his voice down. Clay often told him to stop shouting.

"Did I hear you right?" asked Harper. "You're saying some-body found a corpse at the cemetery?"

"Two corpses, Lieutenant."

Harper tossed a puzzled look to Clay. "There are dead people at the cemetery. Isn't that where they're supposed to be?"

"Not these, Lieutenant," said Kelton. "Some people found them hidden in the brush. Jaime … I mean, Officer Greene told me the bodies are all torn up. It's why he's asking for the coroner and backup."

"What do you think, Johnny?" asked Clay.

Lieutenant Jonathon Harper gathered their paperwork into a neat stack. "I think Kelton should call the coroner and tell him to get to Briar Glade. Then you, me, and Kelton should get in a patrol car and drive out there as well. These timesheets are done anyway, we were just double-checking them."

Clay smiled. "Yes. Timesheets are boring. I like your idea better, Johnny." All three hundred pounds of Inspector Daniel Clay rose from his chair. He gathered his coat and a hat to keep his vast, bald head covered. "Kelton, let's get going."

"Yes Sir!" said Kelton, already running down the hall.

* * *

On their patio, the Trents were sipping pop, smoking their L&M cigarettes, and enjoying the early-evening air. Danny Sherman, Jeff's co-pilot, was coming over tonight with his steady girl, Mirna Thatcher.

They'd made plans for dinner and a movie. Noodles and crabs at the Golden Panda Inn, then off to the Cornell to see Hitchcock's latest, *The Man Who Knew Too Much*.

A police car wailed past the house. "That's not Danny," said Jeff.

"But it *is* the fifth siren in the last hour," said Paula.

"Oh, something's happening down at the cemetery," said Jeff, bending a bottle cap into a taco shape. "Saw it on the way home. Cop cars, red lights spinning."

Paula got on her toes and looked over the fence. "Nothing here, must be on the far side."

"Whatever it is, the morning paper will carry the whole story," said Jeff. "If you're curious."

Paula returned to her wicker chair and retrieved her cigarette from the coral-colored ashtray. Jeff's eyes hadn't moved from the bottle cap turning in his fingers.

"Hey, hi there," she said. Jeff blinked a few times, then looked to her with a little smile. "Seems like you're still up in the clouds."

"Maybe I am."

"I wish you'd come clean, Jeff."

His eyes narrowed. "What do you mean?"

Paula stubbed out her cigarette and walked around behind Jeff's chair. "I know something's wrong. You've been off-kilter since that Chicago run last week. Is there something about the flight?" She reached her arms around his shoulders, laying them across his chest. Her cheek rested against his ear.

They stayed that way for a time, saying nothing. He felt his tensions ease with each breath. Paula was the best thing to ever happen to him. He had to decide, would he keep her protected from the truth or tell her the truth?

"On that flight," said Jeff, "the turnaround from Chicago last week ..."

"Go on," she said.

He stood up and looked at his hands. "Just before we got back to Burbank, I saw a flying saucer." He said it out loud. No going back now.

"A saucer?" She took a moment to consider, to make certain she heard him right. "You mean the kind from up there?"

"Yeah, or its counterpart, 'up there,' I mean. Who can say where it came from?" Jeff paced around his patio. "Danny saw it, too. And Edie. The thing lit up the whole flight deck with a blinding glare. And then some kind of shockwave nearly pushed us off course."

"Jeff, my God," she moved closer. "What happened next?"

"The passengers didn't see it. The saucer kept right in front of the nose, moving with us. Then, as quick as it came, it flew off again."

"Did you report it?" asked Paula. "You must have reported it, right?"

"Yeah," said Jeff. "We radioed Burbank right after we saw it. Mac Robbins was in the tower."

That brought a smile to both of them. She put her hands on his shoulders and sat him down. "Well, at least you got to tell the story to a friend." Paula remembered more. "This is why you were late getting home, isn't it? You were supposed to be here for breakfast, but you barely made it for dinner."

"We got our landing instructions and Mac said he'd ask his superiors what to do. They told us to keep it quiet until landing. Well, as soon as we got off the plane, soldiers escorted us to a van. Parked right there on the tarmac."

"Oh Jeff," said Paula. "Where did you go?"

"They drove us to a building out at Los Alamitos. Took us to a room full of big army brass - for a debriefing. They asked a thousand questions. We didn't get to ask any of our own. Then they made us swear to secrecy about the whole thing."

"And you've kept it inside all this time. Because they made you swear not to tell."

"Yeah, but enough is enough." Jeff stood and rubbed a fist into his palm. "Oh, it burns me up. These things have been seen for years. I've heard the rumors. We made our report, and they weren't even surprised. They had procedures in place - the van, the debriefing. For them, this was all routine."

"There must be something more you can do about it."

"There isn't," said Jeff. "The public ought to know about this. I saw a flying object that can't possibly be from this planet. But I can't say a word. I'm muzzled by army brass! I can't even tell anyone I saw the thing!"

"You told me," said Paula, standing. "It means a lot."

Jeff held her tight. "I'm so sorry, Darling. I shouldn't have kept this from you. Not for a week, not for a minute."

"I'm just glad you're all right," she said. "And if anyone asks, I'll tell them you didn't say a thing."

* * *

Two patrol cars sat parked on the path near the mourners' grisly discovery. The sun had fallen, so the high-beams and spotlights from the police vehicles were the only things providing visibility.

The first officer on the scene, Jaime Greene, stood with Bernard and Shirley Klemens, reviewing their statements. Others swept the area, looking for blood trails, footprints, anything. They worked by flashlight, making it slow going.

As soon as their patrol car arrived, Kelton joined the sweep. Harper stayed by the vehicle, barking into the radio handset. Clay got briefed by the coroner, Derek Hargrove. He'd finished his initial examination moments before.

"It's as bad as anything I've ever seen," said Hargrove. "Their clothes, skin, everything's been shredded by something jagged. An unwavering, ferocious attack. I can't determine the weapon yet. Need to get them to the lab for a proper look."

"You know anything for certain?" asked Clay.

"They've been here for a week, maybe more. And the attack happened someplace else. Not enough blood around this area. They've got no identification on them, and their faces are so damaged I'll need to use dental records for a positive ID."

"You think it might have been an animal?"

"Again, I'll know more after the autopsies, but I don't think so. They were hidden behind the brush and headstones. Placed there and positioned. And even though they're torn apart, nothing is missing. Nothing is … eaten. Doesn't sound like a wild animal to me."

"I was hoping you'd say it was an animal," said Clay. "Because then I wouldn't have to hunt down a maniac."

"I'm doing the examination first thing tomorrow. You'll have my findings before noon." The men shook hands, and Hargrove gathered his notes and gear then headed to his car.

Clay took a hard look at the bodies. Who could do this? And it's a pair of victims. Are there a group of violent murderers out there? Or worse yet, is it one horrifying madman with incredible strength?

He talked with Officer Lawrence Tucker, one of the first on the scene.

"It's just terrible," said Tucker. "Have you ever seen the like?"

"Only in a car crash," said Clay. "Who found them?"

"The man and girl," said Tucker, motioning to the couple talking with Officer Greene.

Lieutenant Harper joined them. "I just got off the radio with the morgue wagon," he said. "They're a few minutes out. The coroner's finished, right? They can transport the remains?"

"Hargrove just left," said Clay. "They can remove the bodies any time."

"Did he have anything to report?" asked Harper.

"Won't know anything certain until the autopsy tomorrow." Clay kept looking at the Klemens. "Have they given their statement?"

"Yeah, much as they could," said Tucker. "They're pretty scared."

"Finding a mess like this ought to make anyone frightened," said Clay. "Cut them loose, we'll call if we need more information. Offer them a ride home in a patrol car if they're too shook up to drive. You got it?"

"On my way," said Tucker. He hurried toward the civilians.

"Johnny," said Clay, "I want you to take charge."

"Okay," said Harper. "What are you gonna do?"

"Look around a little." Clay's instincts tugged him toward the back section of the cemetery.

"All right," said Harper. "There's no lamps or anything along the walking paths. Tucker said it's dark like you can't believe. Once you get beyond the range of our lights you won't be able to see your hand in front of your face."

"Let's hope there's a flashlight left in the patrol car," said Clay.

He found a good one in the trunk. Nice, strong beam. He shined it at Harper. "I'm off," he said.

"You be careful Clay," said Harper.

"I'm a big boy now, Johnny," said Clay. He headed away along the meandering path, backtracking the Klemens' steps.

FOUR

Somebody's Responsible

High over the Pacific Ocean, the saucer soared unnoticed. They were tasked with establishing a scene of operations, a critical step in their plan.

The ship would land at a repeat location, the knoll at Briar Glade Cemetery, even though repetition in flight patterns and coordinates might lead to unwanted detection. Still, the plan had to move forward. Time worked against them. Risks had to be taken.

As it glided past the surf and moved over the land, the alien craft maintained a high altitude, reducing the risk of discovery. As they neared the landing point, the saucer dropped vertically then leveled off at just 500 feet. With a great glow emanating from the gravity aversion engines, the vessel floated low and swift, covering the final miles in seconds. If anyone caught a glimpse of their arrival, the bright lights and backdraft would prevent them from seeing anything in detail.

Behind the same knoll at the Briar Glade Cemetery where it landed a week before, the saucer settled in, became dark and silent. Soon, their experiments could continue.

* * *

The Trents prepared for Danny and Mirna's arrival. In the kitchen, Paula sliced cantaloupe and cheese into cubes. Jeff put paper towels and a bottle of spray cleaner to work on the patio table.

He quickly used up all the paper towels he had. "Are there more of these?" he called, waving the soggy remnants. "It's a lot of dirt."

Paula brought him a whole roll of towels from the kitchen. "I don't want to know what blows over that fence," she said. Then, a blast of light flooded the patio.

The source of the intense illumination crossed into the distance, trailed by a gust that knocked the Trents off their feet.

In another few seconds, all was calm again. Jeff ran to Paula. "Are you all right?" he said.

"Yes, I'm fine. Are you?"

"Yes, all in one piece," said Jeff. "Look, the patio furniture got tossed around."

"Yeah, and so much glare," said Paula, looking to the sky, "So bright. My God, Jeff! Is this the same thing you saw in front of the plane?"

"It's hard to say," said Jeff. "This happened so fast, I only got a glimpse. What did you see?"

"The glow made it hard to see anything. I'm pretty sure flew right over our house and then toward the cemetery."

"I had to shield my eyes," said Jeff. "But the light ... the gust holding us down ... I think it *could* have been another flying saucer."

Paula buried her head in Jeff's chest. "Good Lord. Are they following you?"

"I hope we're wrong. I hope it's something else." He tried to get them moving, to take their minds off the saucer sighting. "C'mon Honey, let's get this patio put back together."

* * *

The morgue attendants had one corpse secured in the van. By the headstones, they lifted the other onto a stretcher.

"Careful where you walk," said Harper.

"You don't have to worry," said Walters, the lead attendant. "We always step into the prints we've already left, so we don't foul the scene."

"That's good," said Harper. "We have to cover the area inch-by-inch once the bodies are clear. We need it undisturbed." A slapping noise drew the Lieutenant's attention. Officer Kelton beat his flashlight against his palm. The bulb flickered and dimmed.

"For corn's sake," said Kelton. "These batteries are done, and I don't think we have any more. How are we supposed to see, Lieutenant?"

As if in answer to Kelton's question, a great object flew overhead and, for just a few seconds, lit the area like a baseball stadium. As soon as it passed, a blast of air pushed everyone to the ground. The morgue attendants lost their grip on the stretcher. Their grim burden rolled across the graveyard.

* * *

In his youth, Inspector Daniel Clay spent a lot of time camping. By the time he was eight years old, he'd been under the stars in every kind of terrain and weather. But he'd never seen a night as dark as this.

Switching on his flashlight revealed space the size of a trash can lid. Switching it off was like closing his eyes. No good. This part of the investigation would have to wait until morning.

As he made that decision, he saw an unexpected shape on the path - his shadow.

The shadow became more defined as a large object projecting brilliance flew overhead. He ducked and covered, a reflex from his army training. It served him well, as the trailing blast of wind would have surely thrown him down.

* * *

Jeff Trent felt a start as another set of lights crossed the patio, but they belonged to a Buick Skylark, not a flying saucer.

Danny Sherman was right on time. "Boy," he said, "lots of police cars at the cemetery tonight."

"We don't know why," said Jeff. "Where's Mirna?"

"Well," said Danny, "I had a date Saturday night."

"Yes?" said Paula.

Danny shrugged. "She found out about it. I think we're through."

"What about this other one?" asked Jeff, laughing. "Miss Saturday Night?"

"Her? She didn't leave a number and she's flown back to Tallahassee." Danny sat down and started popping cheese cubes in his mouth. "When's the reservation at the Panda?"

He got no answer. Jeff and Paula exchanged silent stares.

"We can still go, just us three, right?" asked Danny.

"Are we not going to talk about what happened?" said Paula.

Danny's cheese consumption ceased. "What's this now?"

"A flying saucer," said Paula.

"I thought they warned us *not* to talk," said Danny, shaking his head at Jeff.

"She means another one," said Jeff. He started pacing. "A new one. Here. Tonight." He pointed, "Something flew past, from there to there, about twenty minutes ago."

"The force knocked us down," said Paula. "It knocked the patio furniture over, too."

"Could be anything," said Danny.

"No," said Jeff. "It was bright like the sun, like what you and I saw in front of the plane."

Danny took a few minutes to think. Finally, he asked, "What did you do when this thing flew over?"

"What could we do?" said Jeff. "The exhaust or slipstream or whatever you want to call it, it held us. Kept us on the ground."

"Like the wave that shook the plane," said Danny.

"Just like." Jeff moved to Paula and took her hand. "After we made sure we weren't hurt, we got the patio put back together then you got here."

"If I hadn't seen something like this myself," said Danny, "I'd call you both crazy."

"But you did see it, the one in front of the plane last week, right?" asked Paula.

Danny grimaced. "Those people from the government said we're supposed to keep it under our hats." He shook a finger and spoke in a low voice "'You saw nothing.' They told us, over and over."

"They also gave us a phone number," said Jeff.

"A phone number?" said Paula.

"Yeah," said Jeff. "I've got the card in my bag. Some office in Washington."

"Oh yeah," said Danny. "We're supposed to use it if we have anything else to report."

"Well, I think this qualifies," said Paula. She hopped over to the door and held it open for her husband. "Go get on the horn, Flyboy."

* * *

Once he was sure the flying object had passed, Clay got on his feet. He could see a little better now, the deeper darkness had faded.

He took a few cautious steps along the path, trying to look in all directions at once. He knew the thing landed nearby. He heard engines power down. Then, silence. Not even crickets.

Until a new sound came from everywhere and made him freeze. A whirring tone. When he turned his head, it pitched lower. When he inched down the path, it pitched higher. He drew his police revolver and checked it was fully loaded.

Other noises sprang out. A few yards ahead of him, he heard

movement among the trees. A few yards behind, old, sturdy hinges creaked. That one got his attention.

He crept toward the creaking.

A few minutes earlier he'd passed a vault. It looked different now. The heavy, carved door hung open. He stepped closer to investigate, and the whirring sound deepened.

Movement - off his left shoulder. He spun on it, the flashlight in one hand and the gun in the other, aiming in concert. The beam revealed an old man draped in a black shroud moving slowly toward Clay.

The black cloth covered part of the odd man's face. But not his eyes. They held Clay in their gaze.

Clatter – from behind. Branches snapping. Clay spun again. Just ten yards down the path, a woman with impossibly pale skin reached her long, jagged fingers toward him. She closed the distance with unsteady strides.

This pair had to be the homicidal maniacs who killed those two men. Though each looked frail, they exuded threat. Clay made out more of their features as they came nearer. Severe and twisted. Unnatural expressions, as if sculpted by hands unfamiliar with emotion.

"Hold it, both of you," said Clay. He tried to move away from them, but they countered every step. "Stop or I'll shoot." They kept to opposite sides, splitting his focus, making him turn back and forth.

Their relentless, awkward steps continued. The Inspector had no choice but to fire. He aimed at the man and pulled the trigger, hitting him in the center of his chest. Then, he turned to the woman. "Stop, or you'll get the same," he said.

She didn't stop. Clay shot her, his bullet striking center-mass, same as the man.

But she kept coming. They both kept coming. No change in their pace. No change in their eyes. He fired twice more at the man, each round piercing his heart, but the lunatic shrugged it off.

His last two bullets hit the woman point blank. He saw the impact rattle her gaunt frame, but there was no change in her pace. The unearthly couple reached Clay. They reached into him. Pulled him down and tore at him.

He screamed. Briefly.

* * *

"Get over there, Riley. They need help with the stretcher," said Harper. After the saucer's flyover, it only took seconds for him to take control of the scene again. "You two men, make sure everyone by the van is all right. And where are those civilians? Our witnesses?"

"They left before," said Kelton. "Took their own car."

"We should call their house later and make sure they got home all right," said Harper. "Greene? Jaime Greene!"

"Yes, Lieutenant?" said Greene.

"There you are," said Harper. "Do a head count. You know who's supposed to be here, right?"

"Yes, Sir." Greene started a lap around the scene.

"Kelton! Where's Kelton?" said Harper.

He was still standing next to him. "Yes, Lieutenant?"

"I want you to ride along with the morgue boys. If some other weird thing happens, I want uniform with them."

"You – you want me to – to – to ride with the bodies?"

Harper held onto Kelton's shoulder, tight. "They aren't going to hurt you, Kelton. We're trying to find the ones who hurt *them.*"

Gunshot! An abrupt, unmistakable sound.

Again! Then two more.

"Clay's in trouble," said Harper.

"Bet that apparition we saw had something to do with it," said Tucker.

Every officer on the scene drew their weapon and looked in the direction of the gunfire.

Two more shots echoed through the cemetery. Then screaming.

"Kelton, come with me," said Harper. "You too, Tucker. Everybody else stay here, keep this area secure."

The three men ran down the path, toward the shots they heard moments before. Ahead, they saw a point of light.

"Over there, Lieutenant," said Tucker.

"I see it," said Harper. "Faster!"

The men sprinted all the way to the tiny beacon. It was Clay's flashlight, lying on the ground. His hand rested on top of it.

He was on his belly in the dirt, blood still oozing from his wounds. His neck and face, torn and savaged. His empty revolver lay near his ankle.

Officer Tucker leaned down and checked for a pulse. Kelton walked a small circle, looking for evidence.

"Is he dead?" asked Harper.

"Yeah," said Tucker. He stood and removed his hat. "He's messed up as bad as those two back there. Who could do this?"

"Your guess is as good as mine, Larry," said Harper.

The three men stood for a time, wondering how the division would go on without Inspector Daniel Clay.

"So, what's next?" asked Kelton. "You're in charge now, Lieutenant."

"Yeah, guess I am," said Harper. "Kelton, run back and get on the radio. Tell the coroner he's gotta make another trip out here."

"Got it," said Kelton. "Anything else, Lieutenant?"

"We'll just have to go step by step. Establish a perimeter and look for the attacker," said Harper. "Because one thing's sure. Inspector Clay is dead. Murdered. And somebody's responsible."

FIVE

Saucers Seen over Hollywood

Deep inside the Pentagon, a row of flash folders lay like shingles along the left side of General Harold Roberts's desk. If this morning was anything like yesterday, his ensign would bring more before he got halfway through these.

As head of the Saucer Initiative, his eyes were the only ones authorized to see all the information. Other people knew portions of the intelligence. Roberts alone knew the entirety.

The first folder held a report from California. A small-circulation newspaper, *The Hollywood Chronicle*, ran a headline yesterday reading SAUCERS SEEN OVER HOLLYWOOD. The accompanying article said a carload of people witnessed a saucer flying near the 101 Freeway. At the same time of day, a tourist reported a bizarre, hovering craft to the Hollywood Sheriff's Station. The paper called the sightings "verified" because the two sightings backed each other up.

The article, nested between items on new tax legislation and building codes, had little conjecture or detail. Just a police-blotter approach with a couple of quotes which, frankly, made the witnesses sound like yokels. General Roberts made a few coded notes in his master document and pulled the string on the flash folder.

With a pop and a flare, it vanished. And if anyone asked, it never existed in the first place.

The government had influenced Hollywood into making more films about bug-eyed aliens invading Earth. Discrediting witnesses became simpler with more and more of those pictures in the theaters. "It's just something they saw in a movie."

The saucer incidents involving local police departments couldn't be dismissed as easily. The officers involved were ordered to keep their mouths shut, but would they? And then there was the episode in Virginia. An errant army rocket started a fire in the Cumberland State Forest. More than 50 acres burned, a real black eye for the Saucer Initiative. Luckily, there were no injuries.

With dozens of new reports on his desk every day, it was still Breverton that kept Roberts awake at night. The Joint Chiefs and the CIA ran in perpetual circles creating cover stories, keeping all this from the public. But those stories didn't change the facts.

A few weeks ago, in the skies over Nevada, this business became a shooting war. And not a single member of any agency had acknowledged that fact, even in the most secure setting.

The aliens could wipe us out in minutes if they wanted to. Yet, none of the upper-tier decision makers wanted to mention it.

A month ago, the general gave a standing order to shelve all new ordinance, as recommended by Colonel Edwards. Since then, there had been several engagements and thankfully, those engagements played out like the earlier ones: The saucers broadcast senseless noise over eighteen distinct radio channels while the army fired shells at them. Eventually the aliens retreated.

Most importantly, they didn't use their damn beam weapon again.

Each day, it got harder to keep the lid on. Chatter in the papers, chatter on television. The people reporting these incidents still sounded like crackpots. That was in the government's favor.

But sooner or later a civilian would come forward with real

evidence. Impossible to bury. Impossible to explain away. Then the truth will make this operation unpleasant.

General Roberts's ensign came in, saluted, and apologized for the interruption. "Sir, the tech lab has asked if you can see them. Right now. I have a car waiting."

"Is it those fragments from Breverton? Have they found a weakness?"

"No sir. It's the Language Computer. They think they've cracked it."

* * *

"It's the tenth? You sure today isn't Wednesday?" asked Officer Jaime Greene.

"Sure, I'm sure. It's Thursday the tenth," said Officer Larry Tucker. "Been Thursday ever since midnight last night."

Greene shook his head as he pulled a part-finished form out of the typewriter. "Gotta start again," he said wadding it up. Every cop spent a lot of their time typing out the paperwork.

At the desk facing Greene's, Tucker did the same monotonous job. "I can't remember the last time I got through all my reports without wadding up at least one," he said.

"Ain't it the truth," said Green, rolling paper into the machine. "Still, I think I'm going a little screwy. I keep losing track of time, of days. I swear when I got to the station it was light out, 4:00 on the dot. I checked in, grabbed these forms, and now - boom! It's 6:00. Like I lost two hours."

"We're supposed to be at the Valley Inn around 8:00. You remember that, right?"

He did, and he half wished he didn't. "Yeah. Inspector Clay's wake. I guess everybody but us went to the service today."

"Kelton is your relief. Should be here any time now," said Tucker, tapping on his keys. He could type out a report and carry on a conversation at the same time. "Riley's taking over for me in an hour. I've pulled the dawn shift tomorrow, though. Gonna be rough."

"The Valley Inn is usually a good time, but I don't think it's going to be so good tonight," said Greene. "You know, I keep seeing him with his face in the dirt, all bloody. It's not how I want to remember the man." He hammered out a few more letters. "Hey Tucker, does 'disturbance' end with 'a-n-c-e' or 'e-n-c-e?'"

"It's 'a-n-c-e.'"

"Thanks."

"And you're not alone," said Tucker. "Finding Clay laid out, it haunts me, too. At least there haven't been any more victims."

"Yeah, but no leads, either. No progress. Riley thinks a gang of crazy hobo maniacs did it. Jumped a freight and we'll never see them again." Greene pulled the finished page from his typewriter and reached for a fresh form. "Crap," he said. "I'm out of carbon paper."

"I got lots," said Tucker, pushing a box across his desk. "If it was a bunch of maniacs, they still had to go somewhere. We've been watching the wires, coordinating with other precincts. Nothing like this has happened anywhere else. Did those maniacs suddenly become sane?"

"I think it has something to do with that saucer," said Kelton. For once, he had entered the squad room quietly. He stood at the bulletin board, reading the day's hot sheet.

"Hello Kelton," said Greene.

"Hello Jaime, Larry," said Kelton.

"How was the service?" asked Tucker.

"Lots of people," he said, walking to the coffee urn. "Lots of uniforms. I held myself together pretty well, but when those bagpipes started ..."

"Yeah," said Greene. "That's when everybody starts the waterworks. Really rips you up."

Tucker stopped typing. "Did you say something about a saucer, Kelton?"

Kelton searched around the coffee station for a clean mug.

"Oh, I'm convinced. The light we saw the other night. And the gust. Well, it shoved us all around. It was a flying saucer. I saw this guy on TV talking about them."

"Are you telling me Martians killed our victims?" asked Green. "Like in the movies?"

"Look, you were there, you saw it too," said Kelton, dropping a third scoop of sugar into his mug. "It wasn't a helicopter. I don't care what they're telling us."

Tucker shook his head. "The FAA is a government agency, and if they say it was a whirlybird, that's good enough for me. Plus, the flight logs out of Burbank Airport showed a chopper headed to Castaic."

"Who did you see talking about flying saucers on TV?" asked Greene. "Did Douglas Edwards interview a little green man? Brinkley and Huntly talk with visitors from outer space?" He fed the typewriter and returned to his chores.

"Laugh all you want," said Kelton. "And if you must know, it was Criswell, the fellow on Channel 13. He said there's people all over the country reporting stuff like this, and it's only a matter of time before the aliens make their plans known."

"The psychic guy? Come on Kelton, he's full of banana oil," said Tucker.

"Think whatever you like," said Kelton. "All I know is I can't shake the feeling we're being watched."

* * *

Colonel Edwards thought he'd been to the middle of nowhere before. But this place, a grid reference 167 miles north of Indio, California, made him rethink it. This featureless patch of dirt felt like the moon.

The colonel felt raw. Last night he was in Baton Rouge. He got a call, late, from General Roberts, head of the Saucer Initiative. Fresh orders. Urgent orders.

He was to get to the airfield immediately, and the waiting

plane would take him to 29 Palms outside of Palm Springs, California. From there, he'd spend three hours white-knuckled in a jeep crossing the Mojave Desert.

Now, that jeep ride concluded at a small set of buildings so tanned and worn they blended in with the dirt. A sagging chain-link fence wrapped around them. His driver got waved through the gate and parked just past it.

"Welcome to the Armored Combat Training Area, Colonel," he said.

"I thought this was called 'Camp Irwin,'" said Edwards.

"Changed it a few years back, Sir. But I'm pretty sure a few of the signs still have the old name."

"Just show me where I'm supposed to be, Private." Edwards climbed out of the jeep and lifted his attaché case.

"All I've been told, Sir, is to get you to this spot," said the driver.

"Colonel? Excuse me, Colonel?" A captain approached and they traded salutes. "I'm supposed to give you this, Sir." He handed Edwards a flash folder. Sealed, eyes only.

It contained a hand-written note from General Roberts.

The man who gave you this is Captain Scott Guy. Please observe his operation. Wait for contact from the saucers. Once they leave, I'll need you to come to Washington. Pull the string when you've finished reading this.

Yours, -Roberts

"You're Captain Guy?" asked Edwards, watching the flash folder spark out of existence.

"Yes, Sir."

"Tell me ... other than myself, are you expecting visitors?"

"It's possible, Sir," said Guy. He leaned into the jeep and addressed the driver. "Private, you know where the motor pool is? East side of camp?"

"Yes, Sir," said the driver.

"This vehicle's had a rough time, and so have you. Our mechanics will give this buggy a once-over while you find the mess and get yourself a sandwich or something. Off you go."

And he did. The captain walked Edwards to the latrine. "There are sinks in there, Sir, if you'd like to wash off some of that desert. And the water's always hot."

When Edwards came out of the latrine, he found Captain Guy waiting for him in a different jeep. A cooler in the back had cold bottles of soda, sandwiches, and even a few apples. "We aren't going far, Sir." said Guy. "I'll avoid the bumps while you're eating,"

They rolled out over the sand. "I guess they've shown up here more than anywhere else," said Guy. "Always in daylight, always from the east. But we never know when."

Edwards finished off one of the sodas along with a sandwich. "Thanks for the chow, Captain. Didn't realize I was so hungry."

"No problem, sir. Chow is pretty good out here, considering how remote we are. Destination is in view now." A cluster of man-made shapes in the distance was the only thing that interrupted the flat desert landscape for miles.

"So, there's no timing pattern?" asked Edwards. "No pulse to their visits?"

"Nothing I know of, Sir. They've been here six times in the last month, but there's no saying when or if they're coming again. So, we wait and watch."

The jeep parked among other vehicles and a few Quonset huts. Edwards clocked the area. A control tower stood to the north, but he saw no airfield. Nearby, banks of T-66 rocket launchers, with 24 tubes each, waited to be loaded. Behind them, rows of half-tracks weighed down with M-16 rockets. Past those, two tank battalions were lined up, staffed, and ready as well.

"Tell me Captain," said Edwards, "if your visitors do show up, what happens?"

"As soon as there's a confirmed visual, we spin this gizmo." The captain pointed at a stack of technology mounted on the back of a truck. The colonel didn't recognize the device. A tall shaft topped with dish antennas rigged to rotate. Control beds surrounded the base, and the unit had its own generator.

Great, thought Edwards. *The eggheads at Vandenberg have created a Buck Rogers barber pole.*

Captain Guy walked him around the mechanism. "There are tape reels under the shielding, recording as the top part turns. An alarm sounds when we have to change those out."

"What does it all mean, Captain?"

"I don't have any idea. Not supposed to. Maybe they want to capture the sound of the saucer's engines. Might be a new sonar system. Who can say? I'm not here to figure it out. I'm here to follow my orders."

"And what are those orders?" asked Edwards.

"I'm supposed to keep the gizmo spinning when there's saucers around and make sure the reels don't spool empty. The three engineers sitting next to the van over there can repair any mechanical failure. The van has enough spare parts and tools to build another one of these things from the ground up."

The colonel pointed out the tanks. "There's a lot of armor."

"Ever since Breverton we've had rockets and tanks on standby, Sir. Basic rounds."

Edwards went sharp. "And just what do you know about Breverton, Captain?"

Guy had stumbled. And he knew it. "Um," he said. "What's a Breverton?"

"That's a fine answer." Edwards cracked a little smile. "But I saw you there. You saw me there. You handed a small case to Major Carlson."

"Yes, Sir. My team found those fragments in the debris area. Made our metal detectors go haywire. After the site closed up, I got promoted. Now I look for things in the sky instead of the dirt."

A siren ramped up. Captain Guy called the observation tower on his walkie. "Klein? Tell me everything. Over."

Edwards overheard the response. "To the east, coming in fast. Flying level at twelve hundred feet. Over." A private appeared and handed the colonel a helmet and binoculars, then disappeared again.

"There, Colonel. You can see them reflecting the sun."

Through the binoculars, Edwards saw two saucers coming his way. How in blazes did General Roberts know they'd be here?

The tanks rolled into formation. Crews loaded the rocket launchers. Guy watched the device turn as his engineers read its gauges and scribbled on clipboards.

The saucers came to the first row of tanks and stopped, hovering at 115 feet. Klein, in the tower, called on all channels and over the PA for everyone to hold their positions.

"Is this typical behavior for them?" asked Edwards.

"Yeah," said Guy. "A trio last time, though. They stayed there for about fifteen minutes, then they buzzed the tower and left."

BOOM! A shell sailed toward the saucers. It exploded just in front of them.

"No. No, no," said Guy. The saucers circled the tank battalions. "Dammit!"

The aliens returned to their positions and hovered, but at half the altitude. "What happens now?" asked Edwards.

"Klein will be on the wire reporting to command. That damned tank."

The walkie burst with orders and counter signs. All the rockets fired. All the tanks fired. Everything got reloaded. And everything fired again.

The saucers remained in place as ordinance split and flashed all around them.

Edwards leaned close to Guy and shouted. "You're certain. They aren't using any new rounds. No splinters? No sonics?"

"Absolutely not, Sir. Out here, we only get the old stuff."

The alien vessels were unharmed. Unmoved. Edwards had seen this play out many times before. Too many. The order to cease fire came after the third volley of shells and rockets. By the time the smoke cleared, the saucers had zipped away, vertically. A mile in just a few seconds, then they dashed off to the east.

Out of nowhere, a tight formation of recon jets flew after them.

"Dammit. It didn't have to go this way!" said Guy. He turned and called to his engineers. "Did you people get what you needed?" They did a final check on the device and their notes, then the lead gave a thumbs-up. "Great. That's great. I'm very happy." He leaned into the walkie. "Klein, you all right up there? Over."

"Everyone's okay," said Klein. "Just some papers flying around. Over."

"That first shell, came from one of the M48s," said Guy. "Did you see which? Over."

"No. But I'll ask around. Over and out."

Edwards put a hand on Guy's shoulder. "Easy, Son."

"We can't get jumpy here," said Guy, calmer. "Whoever fired the first round probably outranks me, but they ought to be rotated home. I don't have to tell you, Colonel; we can't have cowboys. It's too dangerous."

"The higher echelon keeps burying the threat level," said Edwards. "Makes it easy for the men on the line to get cocky. That story they made up about the gas explosion at Breverton, it hides the saucer's capabilities. Brass called it an 'incident.' Well, Breverton wasn't an incident, it was a town. A small town, I'll admit. But nevertheless, a town of people. People who died."

"This area is listed as a targeting range," said Guy. "Mortars, tanks, and rockets. They'll call this 'practice fire.'"

"With everyone aiming skyward. Was it practice fire at the clouds?"

The same private who brought a helmet for Edwards reappeared. "Communique for you, Captain," he said. He traded salutes with the colonel and Guy, avoiding eye contact with each of them as the captain snatched at the note.

"Cripes, Walters, just give me the damn thing," he said. "Everyone can see you know how to salute."

"He does it very well," said Edwards. "Dismissed."

"Sir, yes Sir." The private ran off.

Guy reviewed the note. "We need to get you back to 29 Palms, Sir. You have a flight waiting."

"Thought so," said Edwards. "Anything else?"

Yes," said Guy. "It looks like we've beat them off again. The jets have lost them, and we can't find them on radar. Like they were never here."

"Where the hell do they go?" asked Edwards. "And what's their next move?"

SIX

Plan Nine

Ganymede disliked Space Station Seven. He preferred the Great Tower on their home world. He had pleasant quarters there, one of the many perks he enjoyed as the Ruler's attendant. But this station's proximity to the Epsilon system made it an ideal base of operations for their current affairs. Hopefully, this situation wouldn't last.

It had been a trying week for Ganymede. The Ruler's appointments ran back-to-back, with frequent overlaps. Keeping things moving forward took a great deal of concentration and energy. This rude business in the Epsilon system had become uncontrollable, and it might grow even worse if the principals didn't get their time with the Ruler.

And yet, when word arrived that Commander Eros was coming to the station with news of his Earth mission, the Ruler said, "I shall require a meeting with him. As near to his arrival as possible."

The Ruler insisted on bumping the Ardavian Council to see Eros. That meant moving much of the afternoon's business into tomorrow, and what then? The entire calendar may collapse.

And who will be blamed? Ganymede.

The report Eros sent ahead contained every detail the Ruler

had requested. So why have this meeting at all? Ganymede wondered how a trivial planet like Earth merited so much attention. There were far greater issues elsewhere.

The televisor lit up. An underling was calling. "Apologies, Ganymede," she said.

"What is it, Hebe?"

"Commander Eros just arrived. All three of his ships are docking for regeneration."

"Excellent. Instruct him to meet me in the antechamber as soon as he's cleared. And he is to bring his Second, Tanna, as well."

"It will be done," said Hebe. The televisor went dark.

If nothing else, Eros and his team were punctual, unlike those apes from Ardavia.

* * *

Excerpt from *EARTH REPORT 287: COMMANDER EROS*

...to reiterate, any of the Ten Plans may be implemented if a planet's leaders respond with violence and/or denial. The purpose of each plan is the same, to create a situation the population and its leadership cannot ignore. A revelation of our capabilities.

The chosen plan, if successful, will force said leaders to listen to our warnings.

If the chosen plan fails, annihilation must be considered.

My analysis follows.

The Ten Plans

Plan 1: Infiltrate Population

Not viable. From nation to nation, and in some cases from neighbor to neighbor, Earth people are distrustful of one another and filled with animosity. For Plan 1 to succeed, we would need to replace the entire population.

Plan 2: Weather Control

Not viable. No populations on this world are using any technology for weather control, choosing advances in shelter instead. With no system in place to sabotage, Plan 2 would require establishing such a system.

Plan 3: Technological Interdiction

Not viable. Technological achievements vary in progress and value from culture to culture, with some regions lacking technology altogether. This makes the impact of Plan 3 difficult to predict.

Plan 4: Disease Circulation and Cure

Plan 4 is viable. All humans share biological traits. Further study is needed to determine the best approach.

Plan 5: Mind Control over World Leaders

Not viable. The humans are suspicious of each other, and this extends to their own leadership, making Plan 5 unlikely to succeed. Most leaders have checks and balances built into their seats of power. Any changes to their thinking would be suspect. In some cases, this would likely result in the removal of said leader.

Plan 6: Pose as Deity

Not viable. Though most of the population believes in a deity, they don't believe in the same one. Thousands of deities are currently worshipped, making Plan 6 impossible.

Plan 7: Mutate Food Supply

Not viable. There are certain crops that all populations consume. However, food is not evenly distributed across the planet. Such a disruption in the food supply would possibly wipe out certain populations while leaving those with vast storage or better alternatives relatively stable.

Plan 8: Seismic Disruption

Plan 8 is viable. The seismic activity must be minor and precise, as most structures are not designed to withstand even small tremors.

Plan 9: Resurrection of the Dead

Plan 9 is the most viable. Death is universally feared and misunderstood on this planet. They go to great lengths to deny their own mortality. Our advances in reanimation would be impossible to ignore and have a great impact. Study is needed to find the limits of said advances with this species.

Plan 10: Tidal Displacement

Not viable. The planet is mostly water. The results of Plan 10 would be too difficult to control.

END EXCERPT

* * *

Waiting for Eros and Tanna's arrival gave the Ruler a few minutes of solitude in his chamber offices. Normally this area stayed roomy and neat. Today, reports and devices covered every surface. He reviewed the documentation on the Earth mission. Ganymede, his attendant, had done a stellar job of summarizing the findings.

Eros had taken the initiative to suggest one of the Ten Plans. A sound decision, but he needed authorization to proceed.

The Ruler's attendant would no doubt be annoyed by this last-minute change of schedule and the resulting delays. But if the Epsilon system fell into chaos, there may not be another opportunity to see Eros for some time. Better to finish this here and now. To be done with it.

Done with Earth. In all aspects, the Ruler found the planet contrary.

The civil war in the Epsilon system had spilled over into neighboring regions. Alliances formed. Armadas gathered. Raiding parties terrorized the space lanes. This situation had been brewing for centuries and now, every outcome looked horrid.

Eros had one of the best minds in the service. A shrewd negotiator and brilliant tactician. His Second, Tanna, was equally capable. This Earth mission would seal her promotion to Commander, then she'd have ships of her own.

The Ruler needed them to resolve the trouble on Earth quickly. The pair may be needed in Epsilon, and soon.

The great curtains parted, revealing Ganymede. He stepped into the chamber and crossed his arms over his chest.

"Commander Eros has returned from Earth," he said.

"Good, good," said the Ruler, picking through stacks of reports and forms. Ganymede stepped to the workstation and motioned toward a set framed in green.

"These, Excellency," he said.

"Thank you." The Ruler grasped his attendant's wrist firmly.

"You are making these Epsilon negotiations possible for me. I do appreciate it, Ganymede."

The attendant simply bowed.

"Please," said the Ruler, "send them in."

Ganymede held the curtain to one side, and Eros and Tanna entered. They each crossed their arms over their chest. They must have been exhausted after the long trip from Earth, but both stood tall. Their satin uniforms looked clean and tidy. Excellent, disciplined soldiers.

"Welcome!" said the Ruler. "We don't have much time. Ganymede, please make my apologies to the Ardavians. Let them know I won't be long."

"It will be done," said Ganymede. He left the chamber, hoping the Ruler's time estimate would be uncharacteristically correct.

"I've read your report, Eros," said the Ruler. "Is there anything to add?"

"We are here at Space Station Seven for regeneration," said Eros. "We will return to the planet Earth immediately thereafter."

"Is there any progress?" asked the Ruler. "Any communication?"

"We have attempted every form of contact with Earth's leaders. They deny our existence in public and fire on our ships in secret."

The Ruler shook his head. "It's like Verkassis, all over again."

"Let's hope not," said Tanna. "There is so much potential on this planet." She felt Eros eyeing her. As his Second, she had spoken out of turn.

"All may share their thoughts freely here," said the Ruler. "You know this, Eros. Why do you bristle at Tanna's words? Do you disagree about Earth's potential."

"I apologize, Excellency. I do agree, Tanna is correct. But there is something about these people. Their aggression, their hubris. At times, my objectivity becomes strained."

"You must maintain control," said the Ruler. "You've chosen a plan?"

"Plan Nine," said Eros.

"Plan Nine deals with the resurrection of the dead," said the Ruler, referencing his documents. "Long-distance stasis beams shot into the pineal and pituitary glands of recent dead, not a trivial process. However, I agree with your findings. This plan is the most viable. Have you made any attempts at reanimating an Earth being?"

"Yes, Excellency," said Eros.

"Were you successful?"

"We have risen two so far. The beams have excellent range and, so far, the decedents are responding well. In fact, while testing ambulation on our first subject, two living humans interrupted the experiment."

"What happened?" asked the Ruler.

Eros gave a nod to Tanna. "The encounter was simple to manage," she said. "The living Earth people became unreasonable, panicked at the sight of a walking corpse."

"Precisely our goal," said the Ruler. "Continue."

"The beam controlling our female subject had an affect on the minds of the living. It put them on edge, even before they saw her."

"As our decedent neared the Earth people," said Eros, "the beam's energy became more pronounced. They experienced disruptions in their sense of time and place. This merits further study."

"I should say so," said the Ruler.

"We sent an 'attack' command to our subject," said Tanna. "She used her phalanges as weapons. The Earth people have thin hides, and with our systems overdriving her strength, the dead one easily dispatched the witnesses. They were hidden away, and their deaths will likely be attributed to a wild animal."

"We reanimated a male decedent, as well," said Eros. "Equal success."

"What of the local population?" asked the Ruler. "Is there any suspicion of your movements?"

"We had to dispose of one policeman," said Eros. "However, none of those risen have been seen. At least, not by anyone who still remains alive."

"It's too bad it must be handled this way, but it must," said the Ruler. "Those who we take from the grave will lead the way for our other operations."

The Ruler pressed his palm against the forms framed in green, leaving his mark upon them. "Plan Nine is hereby authorized for full implementation. You need not ask for interim approvals, simply move forward. But do send an updated report in two Earth days."

Eros and Tanna stood tall and crossed their arms over their chests. "It will be done," they said in unison, and left the chamber.

The Ruler took a few sips from his cup of replenisher fluid. With a deep breath, he gathered his thoughts, pawed through the files on his desk, and toggled on the televisor. "Ganymede," he said, "please bring in the Ardavians."

SEVEN

Don't Worry About Me

In full uniform with his bag in hand, Jeff Trent stepped onto his patio. He'd been dreading this next flight. Three days away from home. Burbank to Las Vegas to Albuquerque to San Francisco to Chicago with layovers and overnights along the way.

"I still think you ought to stay with your mother until I get back," he said.

Paula sat in the wicker chair, reading *Look* and fiddling with her cigarette. "All the way out in Santa Monica? No thank you."

"That's not the point."

"That's all the point there's going to be," She stood and wrapped her arms around Jeff's middle. "Besides, don't most men try and *keep* their wives from moving back home to Momma?"

"I didn't say 'move back home,' I just meant -"

"I know what you meant, and I love you for it," said Paula. "But now it's time to go fly your flying machine. Oh, and if you cross paths with another saucer, can you ask them to pick a different house to buzz?"

They kissed. "You got it," said Jeff.

"You be careful," said Paula. "And don't worry about me."

"I'll try," said Jeff. He held her tighter. "But even if I don't think about the saucers, there's still something going on in the cemetery, and that's too close for comfort."

"Listen to me, Flyboy." She put her palms on either side of his head and gently aimed it skyward. "The saucers are up *there*."

Next, she turned his face toward the fence. "And the cemetery's out *there*."

Giggling, she spun him around until he looked toward the patio door. "But I'll be in *there*. Safe in *our house*. Doors locked tight." With another spin, she planted a kiss on his neck. "Now off to your wild blue yonders."

"You promise? You'll lock the doors immediately?"

"I promise. Besides, I'm beat," she said. "I'll be in bed before half an hour's gone, with your pillow beside me."

"My pillow?"

"This probably sounds silly, but it smells like you," said Paula. "Sometimes when it gets a little lonely, I swap my pillow for yours. Nuzzle it. Maybe I'm part wolf."

"Maybe you're part crazy." He grabbed his bag and darted to the car.

Paula hollered after him, laughing. "Crazy huh? The moon's going to be full when you get back. I might just eat you up!"

"I do love you, Darling. See you Thursday." Jeff climbed into their Plymouth convertible, started the car, and waited. After a few moments, he called to her again. "You know I'm not leaving until you're inside."

"All right. If you're especially nice I may even lock the side door." Paula went into the house and made a loud pageant out of turning the lock.

* * *

The three alien saucers held a tight formation as they rushed through space toward Earth. Eros took in Jupiter as it passed over the observation dome of his ship's control deck. A marvelous looking planet. This view always lifted his spirits.

Soon, they'd reach Earth, and his ship would land surreptitiously near the cemetery once again. His support vessels were bound for other locales. They'd broadcast warning messages with every means at their disposal.

Hopefully, the broadcasts would garner a response and make Plan Nine's implementation unnecessary. Still, he needed to be ready. In order to implement the plan on a global scale, these next tests were crucial.

The hatch slid open, and Tanna joined him on the control deck.

"The subjects are doing well," she said. "Both of them are stable. Decomposition is in stasis thanks to our rays. And the old one is showing just as much strength and agility as the younger one."

"Yes," said Eros. "They slow with age because of pain. If it is eliminated, they can fulfill most commands."

"I feared His Excellency wouldn't take our report so well," said Tanna.

"If we were dealing with any planet but Earth, I think his reaction would have been completely different. He understands the difficulties of the Earth race."

Tanna checked the flight controls. "Nearly there. What do you think our next obstacle will be?"

"As long as the Earth people can think, we'll have our problems. At least there will be no obstacles with our test subjects. They cannot think. They are the dead. Brought to a simulated life by our stasis beams."

"I see your point," said Tanna.

"Even though the Earth people can think, they are frightened by those who cannot: the dead," said Eros. "It is just another example of their primitive outlook."

Tanna caught the last glimpse of Jupiter through the dome above. "If only they could see from here," she said. "Their sole point of view is from the surface of their world. That limited perspective creates arrogance. For them, the land and waters of

Earth are everything. So, having climbed their highest mountains and crossed their widest seas, they think themselves kings."

"You're right," said Eros. "The view from space makes it clear; your entire world is a tiny place. You stand on one of billions of planets, surrounded by emptiness. You are living on a spec, drifting in a vast cosmic sea. Insignificant."

"Space makes one humble," said Tanna. "Should this trifling world be allowed to destroy everything? The question itself is foolish. Almost as foolish as the Earth people who have forced us to ask it."

* * *

The cockpit of American Flight 471 was all business tonight. No conversations. No jokes. It made Danny Sherman restless. "You're mighty silent this trip, Jeff," he said.

"Huh?" Jeff Trent was elsewhere.

"You haven't spoken ten words since takeoff," said Danny.

"I guess I'm preoccupied."

"We've got thirty-three passengers back there that have time to be preoccupied. Keeping this flybird on course doesn't give you the opportunity."

"I guess you're right," said Jeff.

"There's nothing wrong at home, is there?"

"Oh no. Everything's all right."

Danny made a few notes in the flight log. "Good. Everybody else I know is splitting up."

"Not a chance," said Jeff. "I'm worried is all. She's there alone."

"Has anything weird happened since the night I was over?"

"No. That flying searchlight hasn't come back. Still has me rattled, though. And there's all that police business at the cemetery, too."

Tray in hand, Edith Packer entered the flight deck. She

reached for the empty plates from the pilots' meals. Jeff handed them to her with a smile and a nod.

"Well, maybe they haven't figured out those crazy skybirds yet," said Danny, "but I give you fifty-to-one odds the police have figured out that cemetery thing by now."

"I hope so," said Jeff.

A bright grin popped onto Danny's face. "And hello, Edie!"

"Hi Silence," she said. "I haven't heard a word from this end of the plane."

"Well, up to a few minutes ago, Jeff was giving me a study in silence."

She teased them with a scolding. "You boys ain't feuding?"

"Not at all," said Jeff.

"Hey Edie, how about you and me balling it up in Albuquerque?" asked Danny. The lady he usually saw there was out of town. He and Edie got too deep into a bottle of gin once and ended up having a clumsy fling. It didn't last. But every now and then he took a shot. Edie didn't like it.

She half-wanted to tell him off but decided to keep it peaceful instead. "Albuquerque?" she said. "Have you read the flight schedule?"

"What about it?"

"They roll up the streets right after sunset," she said, shifting her tray to her hip. "We don't land in Albuquerque until four in the morning."

Danny had a plan. "I've got a friend who runs this after-hours place."

She cut him off. "Let's take care of Jeff's problem first, okay Danny?"

"Jeff's problem?"

"When I walked in," she said. "I heard you talking about Paula."

"I know worrying doesn't help anything," said Jeff, "but I can't get it out of my head. I just want to know she's all right."

"Why don't you radio in and find out? Mac is in the tower," said Edie. "He can call Paula then relay the message for you."

"Hey," said Jeff. "I hadn't thought of that."

"I'd be nervous, too," said Edie. "I read about all this cemetery business. Told you kids not to get a house near one of those places. We get there soon enough as it is."

"He thought it'd be peaceful there," said Danny. "You know, quiet."

"It's quiet alright, like a tomb," said Edie. She watched Jeff's expression fall, saw him blame himself for putting Paula in danger. Time to change the subject. "Say, I almost forgot what I came in here for. How's the coffee situation?"

"Yes, please!" said Danny. "That's for me."

"It sure wouldn't hurt anything," said Jeff.

"Okay, I'll be right back. And Jeff, make that call." She started her turn toward the main cabin but felt Danny's hand on her arm.

"Hey Edie," he said. "I didn't get an answer. How about our Albuquerque ball?"

This guy, she thought, *he never gives up.* "Sorry, Danny. By the time I get those thirty jamokes off the plane, all I'm going to be good for is some shut-eye. You boys behave yourselves and I'll be back with the coffee."

She stepped out and silence returned to the flight deck. Danny did his best to pretend he hadn't been dismissed.

"Hey Danny," said Jeff, batting his eyes. "Why don't you ever ask *me* to the ball?"

"Shut up, Jeff," said Danny.

* * *

Tanna finished tuning the twenty-fifth (and final) vid-point on the televisor. An array of screens displayed multiple angles from each of them. They could now observe all activity at their scene of operations.

Eros reviewed his mission protocols. Several questions needed answers.

At what point will decomposition make the subjects inviable?

Is there an optimum muscle mass for a subject corpse?

Will the differing chromosome structures between genders be a factor?

Does age make a subject less suitable?

Their first set of test subjects were ideal. Each a different gender, plus a decades-wide difference in their ages. The time had come to put them through their paces.

"Tanna," said Eros, "I wish to begin. Are the vid-points calibrated?"

"The televisor is ready," she said. "There are views covering every place they can go."

"Excellent."

Outside their saucer, away from any living Earth people, Eros sent the pair of dead humans into the cemetery. He'd begin with simple tasks. Navigating to a predetermined point. Moving in tandem. Lifting objects. Finding cover.

The dead responded well to the commands, and the beam controlling them had considerable range.

"I've had a thought," said Eros. "The policeman, the one we had to eliminate, how do you feel about making him a test subject?"

She'd been thinking the same thing. "He meets the protocols. Recently deceased, and strong. However, we've never processed such a large specimen, on any planet."

"All the better for the testing," said Eros. "His bulk will take our ambulation and balance probes to their limits."

"His major muscle groups sustained significant damage in the attack. They may no longer function," said Tanna, settling in front of the reanimation console. "But I agree. If this specimen can be controlled, can be useful with all those faults, the results will raise our confidence."

"Excellent," said Eros.

"It will be done," said Tanna. "Time is needed, but he will rise before long."

"Take all the time you need," said Eros, adjusting toggles and knobs on a panel. "I'm going to see how the old man handles a complex string of commands. That nearby home is within the beam's range. He will enter it."

* * *

Just as she had predicted, Paula fell asleep soon after her husband left for the airport. She ate a little something, got into her night-clothes, and climbed into bed with her copy of *Peyton Place.* For three nights running she'd nodded off on the same page. Tonight, she was determined to get to the next chapter.

She failed.

Two hours later, the phone woke her. For a moment, she wondered why Jeff didn't answer it. Her eyes jumped open with the realization he was gone. She grabbed the receiver and sat up.

"Hello?" Her shoulder hurt. *Peyton Place* was a great book, but it made a terrible pillow. "Who's this?" she asked.

"It's Mac, Mac Robbins. Did I dial right? That's you, Paula, isn't it?" He spoke over aircraft noise, beeps, and other voices.

"Oh, hello Mac," said Paula. "What's all that noise? You aren't in the tower, are you?"

"I am, sorry. I've only got a minute. I'm calling for Jeff."

Her thoughts jumped to flying saucers. "Is anything wrong?" she asked.

"No, no. Nothing's wrong. He asked me to call and check in on you."

She smiled and held Jeff's pillow to her chest. "That man," she said. "I told him not to worry about me."

Mac laughed. "And when did Jeff ever do as he was told?"

"Well, his heart is in the right place, I guess," said Paula. "Please tell Jeff I'm fine. In fact, I was asleep."

"Oh, I'm sorry, Paula."

"Well, you didn't know. I feel bad your work got interrupted."

"That's not a problem," said Mac. "I'll radio Jeff and tell him everything's aces over there. Good night, Paula."

"Okay Mac," she said. "Thanks for calling. And my best to Alma. Goodnight." She hung up the phone then put her book on the nightstand. "I guess I'll catch up with Allison MacKenzie tomorrow."

Her ears rang with a constant, whirring sound. It might have been the light bulb. They make noise sometimes when they're going to go. She reached to turn off the lamp and noticed a shape. A man, a tall man draped in black, stood at the window.

No. *In front* of the window. This man was in the room.

He moved toward her.

* * *

The dead subjects had no cognitive ability. No thoughts. No memory. Bodies function as tools, with the beam stimulating glands and firing neurons. Tricking the brain into triggering muscles. Automated systems provided a cascade of signals, operating the corpses.

Eros found their progress pleasing. The old one responded to the "hunt" command with no adjustments needed. He entered the house after forcing the lock on the side door, then moved quietly and found the female resident. On the televisor, the commander watched her react and flee.

He issued a new command: "Pursue."

Moving from one vid-point to the next, Eros tracked Paula Trent as she ran through her house and onto her patio. Though ahead of her pursuer, she wasted time turning in circles, panicking, unclear where to go. Had the beam caused confusion in this Earth person, as it had with the others? Or did this species always fail when presented with things they can't explain?

* * *

Running barefoot through the graveyard, Paula's mind raced. Wasn't she just in bed? It could have been day or night, she didn't know. One thing she did know - she had to get away from the man in the black shroud. He dogged her every step.

Branches and the corners of tombstones caught her night dress, scratched her skin. Her feet were torn and numb from the cold. But she had to keep going. Had to escape.

The small cluster of crosses on her left, and the tree with a large angel statue in front of it … she'd run past them before. Several times. And that noise, the loud whirring, it kept getting louder.

The tall man in the shroud appeared in front of her, blocking her way. He moved toward her. She spun.

Running barefoot through the graveyard, Paula's mind raced. Wasn't she just in bed? It could have been day or night, she didn't know. One thing she did know - she had to get away from the man in the black shroud. He dogged her every step.

* * *

"She's beginning to tire," said Tanna. "And the policeman is ready to rise." The control panel for the reanimation systems had every light blinking.

Eros switched to a vid-point on the other side of the cemetery. Below a tombstone inscribed *Daniel Stellan Clay*, the dirt and leaves shook. Heaps of soil forced their way upward.

"There's no question, he is reacting to the beam," said Eros. "But there is a great deal of soil holding him down."

"Yes, but look how it moves aside," said Tanna. Thick finger-tips broke the surface of the grave. "There. He's made it."

Unsteady, massive hands dog-paddled through the dirt surrounding him. His legs scissored, and his shoulders rocked. And inch by inch, the corpse of Daniel Clay struggled out of the ground.

Slowly, he walked away from his resting place, clumps of dirt falling from his suit. A few moments later, some of the earth he drove from the ground caved back in. His undermined tombstone shifted, then tumbled into the grave.

A grave without a body, and nothing to mark it.

"His bulk moves surprisingly well," said Eros. "We'll have him join the old one." The commander moved three of the knobs on the control panel.

Tanna checked the other views. "Where is our other subject? The dead woman?"

"Here on screen 11," said Eros. "She is near the gate, blocking escape."

* * *

Paula fell again. She didn't want to get up, but she had to. She rose on uncertain legs and leaned against the fence, just for a moment. Just to breathe. Wait … the fence! She was against the fence. With an awkward push, she climbed over it.

She fell on the other side and hit hard. But she had to ignore it, get up and move again. It looked like morning. Had she been running all night? Didn't matter. Down there, across the field … a road. That was Fairbanks Road.

Behind her, the man in the shroud leapt over the fence. And another, much larger figure moved toward them from the cemetery.

Two of them now.

Paula ran across the field toward Fairbanks Road.

* * *

"Tanna, see if you can increase our reach," said Eros, mashing buttons.

"It's no good," she said. "The Earth woman is moving out of the beam's range. We won't be able to control our subjects if they follow her."

"We have to try!" Eros had become sharp, emotional. "Take the other two subjects out of phase. We'll focus all our energy on the old man."

Just at the edge of the televisor, Eros spied headlights. A car moved up the road, toward Paula Trent.

* * *

Emil Caulder, a farmer by trade, was well known in the community. His produce stand at Las Palmas Park sold out every weekend. Today, he'd driven all the way to the parts center in Yuma. His tractor needed a new front-end pedestal, and he lost money every day he didn't have one.

Now the pedestal took up most of the space in his Buick Roadmaster's trunk, and in just a few more miles he'd be back home.

He had trouble parsing what his headlights revealed. A woman, running through a field. Running toward his car in nothing but a torn night dress. Not even shoes on her feet.

And damned if he didn't know her. It was Paula Trent.

She collapsed by the side of the road and Caulder's curiosity changed to urgency. He pulled the car up near her and leapt out to help.

"Mrs. Trent?" he called. "Mrs. Trent, is that you? What's wrong?" She was incoherent, out of breath. Nearly unconscious. He looked back along the way she came. A man in black stood staring at them. Further back, in the darkness, a larger figure moved near the fence.

And where did this whirring sound come from?

No time to think about it. He'd read in the paper about abnormal things happening at Briar Glade and there it was, across this field. He put his arms under Paula Trent and got her into the car.

Caulder worked the starter too hard and stalled the car. In his rear-view mirror, he watched the man move toward them. Slow and steady, with his eyes closed, he calmed himself, turned the key, and rocked the pedals. The car roared to life.

With a tug on the gearshift, he mashed down the gas pedal and the Roadmaster took off. The police station was close by, they'd be there in a few minutes.

* * *

Eros looked defeated. Witnesses. Living witnesses had knowledge of their scene of operations.

"I'm calling all three of the test subjects back to the ship," said Tanna. "Authorities will be coming soon."

"Yes," said Eros. "We'll launch once the dead have been deposited in the stasis chamber. We can take cover in the stratosphere until the authorities leave." He tracked their subjects on the televisor, looking for something positive from all this.

"They move well," he said. "Even the big one."

"Yes," said Tanna. "They've covered a good distance. It will take several millicycles for all three to return."

"We can use the time to preset the launch systems," said Eros, moving to the navigation post.

Tanna saw anger in her commander. This planet, these Earth people, they triggered something primitive in him. "It doesn't matter what the Earth woman has seen," she said. "They won't believe her. They never do."

"I agree," said Eros. "These people don't believe their *own* eyes. They certainly won't believe someone else's."

EIGHT

Spook Details

In the tiny kitchen at the San Fernando Police Station, Officer Larry Tucker dried the newly-washed spoons and mugs. He'd finished his paperwork. No calls on the board. Nothing left to do but this bit of clean up, then he just had to wait for midnight, the end of the shift.

Kelton and Greene were on patrol in the cruiser. But they'd be in soon and clock out at the same time.

The front door of the police station swung open and hit the stop hard enough for Tucker to hear all the way in the kitchen. He thought it was Kelton, but the voice hollering across the lobby wasn't his.

"Help! Somebody, you gotta help us!"

Larry still had the towel in his hands as he ran to the front desk. Emil Caulder, eyes and hair wild, held the door and waved the officer outside. "It's Mrs. Trent, Paula Trent!" he said. "She's in the car, c'mon."

Officer Tucker suddenly had a lot to do.

He called an ambulance to the station. Caulder checked out fine, but Paula Trent was in shock. No major injuries, just cuts and bruises. The ambulance took her to County General Hospital for observation.

Caulder stayed at the police station and made out a statement, describing the scene and Mrs. Trent's pursuers. Tucker thought the man smelled boozy. "Have you been drinking, Mr. Caulder?" he asked.

"I got all shook up, so yes," said Caulder. "I had a couple of pops from this flask here while those ambulance people took care of Mrs. Trent."

"And earlier? Were you drinking then?"

"Not a drop. I drove from Yuma and that's a long ways out. Just coffee, that's all. Didn't want to nod off on the road."

"I'm putting this in your statement," said Tucker. "So, it better be true."

"I know what I saw, and it's all true." said Caulder. "A tall man in black, like some kind of spirit. And another one, big guy, near the fence. They ran poor Mrs. Trent into the ground."

Tucker left the farmer in the interview room and phoned Lieutenant Jonathon Harper at home. He read the statement to him.

"Sounds like the maniacs we've been looking for," said the lieutenant. "We've got to move on this. Everyone's shifts are extended. Get a cruiser to the cemetery and have them look for those suspects, for anything suspicious. And tell them to be careful."

"Right," said Tucker.

"I'll get to the hospital and check on the Trent woman," said Harper. "If she's well enough, I'll try for an interview."

"Got it," said Tucker. "And Mr. Caulder?"

"Cut him loose. Wait for me there at the station, and make sure the midnight shift gets to work on this. Once I get there we'll head out to Briar Glade together."

The patrol car carrying Kelton and Greene got a radio call from Tucker. They were dispatched to Briar Glade Cemetery. Greene liked the sound of overtime, but the assignment needed clarification. "Who are we looking for?" he asked.

"One, possibly two suspects," said Tucker. "First is a tall male, dark hair, wearing a loose-fitting black coat or cloak. We've got even less of a description on the other one. Heavy set, that's all."

"Not a lot to go on," said Greene.

"It doesn't matter," said Tucker. "No one is supposed to be there. If you see *anybody*, cuff them and bring them in. If you see *anything* out of the ordinary, flag it. And be careful, they might be Inspector Clay's killers."

* * *

Eros stared at the televisor as if his glaring might make the dead move faster. He leaned into the communication pad. "They'll be at the hatch in a moment," he said. "You can open it now, Tanna."

"I'll let you know the moment they are secured," said Tanna. Over a speaker from two decks above, Eros' voice had an edge. Terse. These humans drew out a harshness in him, one she hadn't seen before.

She opened the hatch. The policeman and the female made their way to the stasis chambers as the voice of Eros rang out again. "Cease their hunting quickly," he said. "They can't tell us from anyone else."

An unnecessary order. Key protocols included shutting down all inputs other than ambulation as soon as the subjects entered the ship. The deceased pair came into the room with Tanna, and she used the precision hand controllers to move them to their tubes. On the televisor, she saw the old one nearing the saucer.

She spoke into the pad. "Two are stowed, Eros. The old one will be secured as soon as he arrives. You've seen the car approaching the gate?"

He hadn't. Too focused on the test subjects' movements. Too focused on his failure to eliminate the witnesses, and the Ruler's potential reaction to his report. And there, clear and sharp on the televisor, a police car with more potential witnesses rolled through the main gate of the cemetery.

"Of course, I've seen it." he said, toggling switches at the navi gation console. "Prelaunch sequence has begun. Alert me as soon as the old one is secure."

"It will be done," said Tanna.

* * *

"It's tough to find something when you don't know what you're looking for," said Officer Jaime Green. He and Kelton walked the main path at Briar Glade. Their flashlights swept the area on either side.

"I don't think the lieutenant does either," said Kelton.

"What do you mean?"

"They told us to 'cuff anyone and flag anything,'" said Kelton. "Doesn't sound like they know what we're after."

"Tell you what I know," said Greene. "I was supposed to be off duty an hour ago."

"What do you want from me? I'm just a hard hat like you."

"Hang on," said Greene. "Shine your light over here." The beams revealed a berm.

"It's dirt," said Kelton. "Just some dirt, piled up."

"They said to flag 'anything,'" said Greene. "Let's check it out."

* * *

Tanna entered the control deck and took her seat at the systems console. "The old one is secure," said Tanna. "We are ready."

"This will be a low-energy launch," said Eros, punching buttons. "No lights. No gusts. They will hear our engines, nothing more."

"Excellent," said Tanna.

Eros flipped the toggles with intent. "I've summoned the other ships. We are going to rendezvous in orbit, then contact Space Station Seven with an update." They were seen at the operations site, and the witnesses still lived. They would need to speak to the Ruler.

* * *

Lieutenant Harper and Officer Tucker parked their unmarked Ford behind a police cruiser at Briar Glade. "We should find Greene and Kelton," said Tucker. "Looks like they're already here."

"Right," said Harper. "The Trent's house is over there, on the far side of the chapel. I'm sure we'll come across the others if we head that way."

As the men moved out, they each felt a vibration coming through the ground. "Earthquake?" said Harper.

"Don't think so," said Tucker. "It's different."

The vibration faded, and a sound rose. A steady pulse, a mechanical chuffing. At first it came out of the south, but quickly grew in volume until the clamor surrounded them. It only lasted for a moment, then faded entirely.

"What do you suppose that noise was?" asked Tucker.

"Well," said Harper, "it's no more strange than the other things happening around this cemetery."

"It might have been a spirit," said Tucker. "Like old Farmer Caulder talked about."

"At this point, I'm open to anything."

Tucker shook his head. "The only spirits he connected with tonight were those I smelled on his breath."

"Don't forget what I told you on the way over. Mrs. Trent claims to have seen the same thing. She didn't have anything on her breath."

"Maybe not," said Tucker, "but with her state of mind, can we believe what she said?"

"It's true, she was frightened," said the lieutenant. "In shock. But don't forget her torn night dress and scratched feet. She wore herself out running away from *someone*, and that's a fact."

"I hadn't thought of it," said Tucker. "I guess it's why you're a detective and I'm still a uniformed cop."

"Sometimes it's only the breaks, Larry. Come on, we should get back to -" The next moment, Kelton and Greene thundered toward them.

"Lieutenant, Lieutenant!" called Kelton. "Did you hear that crazy noise?"

"How could we help it?" said Harper.

Green looked all around, as if the sound's source lurked nearby, watching them. "It sure was strange," he said.

"Know what caused it?" asked Kelton.

"No more than you do," said Tucker.

"If it weren't for orders," said Greene, "I'd get out of here right now."

"The noise came from a saucer," said Harper.

And the officers stopped talking.

Earlier, he'd received a call from high-ranking officials in Washington, D.C. They said his precinct was a hotbed for saucer activity, and they were sending someone from the Pentagon to investigate. This official, identified only as "Colonel," would arrive in the next few days. They told Harper to gather a small group of officers he trusted to assist the colonel with the inquiries.

For Harper, now was as good a time as any to assemble that group. Even if it meant including Kelton. For all his faults, you couldn't question his loyalty.

After a second or two of contemplation, the men started in again.

"Did you say 'saucer,' Lieutenant?" asked Greene. "Like a *flying saucer*?"

To himself, Kelton whispered, "I knew it."

"What makes you say that?" asked Tucker.

"Just think for a minute," said the lieutenant, "Do you remember the noise we heard the other night? The night of Clay's attack?"

Tucker nodded. "Of course, I remember. We got knocked to the ground."

"True," said Harper, "but the sound. Think hard and remember that sound."

"Yeah, they're the same," said Greene. "But what about that blinding light?"

"So, we didn't see a light this time," said Harper. "But the sound is unmistakable. Let's just say I know what I know, all right. Some higher-ups from Washington D.C. have reached out to us for help with this saucer stuff. I'll give you all of the details later on, but for now I need you to keep it under your hats. Don't talk to anyone about it. Wives, best friends, your dear sainted mothers, I mean no one."

Each man nodded. "What's next, Lieutenant?" asked Tucker.

"We investigate the attack on the Trent woman." He turned to Green and Kelton. "Have you two walked the fence line over by Fairbanks Road?"

"Not yet," said Greene.

"We might find footprints over there," said the lieutenant. "Maybe something we can take a cast of."

"Oh, this probably doesn't mean much," said Kelton, "but Jamie and me found a grave that looks like it's been busted into."

"What?" said Harper. "Where is it? Might be important."

Kelton stammered as he got his bearings. "It's, um, it's up along the path here, past the crypt."

"All right," said Harper, waving the men forward. "Show us the way."

Some distance down the path, the four policemen gathered at the pile of the loose earth next to a large hole in the ground. "Look, here it is Lieutenant," said Kelton.

"We didn't touch anything," said Greene. "Found it just like this. You can see, this grave has been disturbed. Somebody dug it up, recently."

"Yeah," said Harper, with a cautious lean for a better look. "It's been broken into, all right."

"I wonder," said Tucker. "If someone dug it up, there should be more dirt than this. A big pile where they shoveled it. This looks like part of the soil caved in. Like a good portion's fallen into the grave."

"Could be," said Harper. "Clear thinking like that will move you out of uniform duty before you know it, Larry. Well, we shouldn't go poking around any further without the permission of next of kin."

"It's going to be hard to determine who to call," said Greene. He aimed his flashlight into the depression. "See it?"

"Look at that," said Tucker. "There's a gravestone down there. Must have tipped in when the soil shifted. Looks like the casket is all busted up, too."

"The writing on the stone is angled away from us," said Harper. No matter how they turned their flashlights, none of the men had a way to see it. "We'll have to go down to find out whose grave it is."

"How?" asked Kelton.

"Simple," said Harper. "You're going down and finding out. Looks like you can get in there on this side, then read the tombstone."

Officer Paul Kelton didn't move. Didn't speak. The others took positions all around, casting their flashlights to illuminate as much of the hole as possible. Kelton moved toward the edge, looking for a foothold.

"Here," said Harper. "Give me your light. You're going to need two free hands." Kelton handed it over and stared into the grave.

"Come on, Kelton," said Greene. "You scared?"

"No," said Kelton. "But why do I always get hooked up with these spook details? Maniacs, flying saucers, graveyards." He shook it off. "Oh, all right. Here we go."

The loose soil made the five-foot descent tricky. Kelton flinched when a trail of grave dirt slipped into his collar and down his shirt. "Larry's right about this casket," said Kelton. "It's in pieces. No sign of a body, though."

After some shifting and cursing, he came eye-level with the tombstone.

"Can you read the name?" asked Harper.

"It's too dark," said Kelton. "Can you give me more light?"

They tried, but it didn't help. "Hang on," said Kelton. He reached into his pocket and tugged a book of matches from behind his Pall Malls. He held two of them together and struck them up. By the flickering, amber light, he read the legend carved into the marble.

A squall of memories came at him all at once. He shook out the flame and leaned back against the wall of the grave.

"Can you read it?" asked Harper. "What's it say?"

"I've been here," said Kelton. "Just a few days back, I was right here. So were you, Lieutenant. This is Inspector Clay's grave. But he ain't in it."

NINE

Shocking Facts

Colonel Edwards had been to the Pentagon a hundred times, but he'd never been down the same set of hallways twice. With more than 6 million square feet of office space, the building was the size of a small city.

This time, he was beneath the main structure. Deep, where the real secrets dwelt. He sat waiting in a small alcove outside the office of General Harold Roberts, head of the Saucer Initiative. They'd met a few times, spoken a few times, but most of their communication came in the form of memos that turned to smoke.

The alcove had a small, round coffee table at its center with four stuffed chairs surrounding it. The table supported an ashtray, a carafe of water, and a stack of paper cups. No staff. No front desk.

The door on the east wall led to the hallway, where he came in. The west wall had another door, unmarked, and it should have led to Roberts's office. But in this obscure section of the building, it might go anywhere.

The flight from 29 Palms to Washington, D.C. included a six-hour layover at Fort Riley, Kansas. It gave Edwards the opportunity to lay down in an actual bunk for the first time in days. He managed to sleep for three of those hours and spent the rest of the time trying to figure out how Roberts knew those saucers were coming.

Captain Guy said he had no idea when or if the saucers would return. Yet, a dusty jeep ride got Edwards to the site right on time for the show.

Maybe they had a breakthrough. Maybe it meant they were close to ending this madness.

The unmarked door opened, and General Roberts leaned into the alcove. "Come in, Colonel Edwards," he said.

"Thank you, Sir." Edwards picked up his omnipresent attaché case and came through the door. The general had already returned to his modest desk. Hastily, he tucked folders into drawers, out of sight.

"Close the door, please," he said. "And have a seat."

There were only two chairs in the room, one on each side of the desk. Both the same model, standard military high-back swivel.

As he sat down, Edwards gave the room a quick scan. It looked like the general hadn't occupied this space for long. Banker's boxes stacked up in a corner. Creased maps and star charts taped up on the walls. Models of aircraft and prototype rockets dotted shelves weighed down with ledger books and binders. Everything looked thrown together, not the usual Pentagon standard of neatness.

"Colonel," said Roberts, "I understand you witnessed a saucer encounter at Camp Irwin."

"Not quite," said Edwards. "It's got a new name, the Armored Combat Training Area."

"Really? Wish they'd tell me these things."

"Well, no matter what they're calling it, I did observe a saucer encounter there."

The general tapped his fingers on a folder. "So, you believe there are such things as flying saucers, Colonel?"

"Yes, Sir." Edwards knew where this was going. These questions had to be asked. Roberts had to hear the colonel affirm his understanding of the layers of secrecy surrounding the Saucer Initiative.

"You understand," said the general, "there's a government directive stating there is no such thing as a flying saucer?"

"I do understand. It's a directive I quote often."

The finger tapping ceased. "Do you stand by your statement? Have you seen flying saucers?" asked the general. "Keep in mind, this could mean a court-martial. You'd be opposing the directive."

Edwards took a breath, then leaned forward. "General Roberts," he said. "may I speak freely?"

Roberts brought his hands together. "You may."

"How could I hope to hold down my command if I didn't believe in what I saw and shot at?" He let the question hang in the air.

The general pulled a Kent cigarette from its crush-proof box and lit it with the black crackle Zippo he'd had since the war. "I like you, Colonel," he said. "And there *are* flying saucers. There's no doubt they are in our skies. They've been there for some time."

"What're we going to do about them?"

"That's why you're here," said Roberts. He opened the topmost folder on his desk. "Let's start with Jeron Criswell King, also known as The Amazing Criswell."

Edwards had never heard of anyone named Criswell, amazing or otherwise. Roberts passed him copies of *Spaceway Magazine*, syndicated newspaper columns, and transcripts of television programs all featuring the man's outlandish predictions.

To the colonel, this seemed like a gag. "I'm not following, Sir," he said. "Why is the Initiative interested in this person?"

"Because lately, he's been talking about saucers. Writing about them, too. Look here." The general passed a brief across the desk. Excerpts with Criswell reporting on saucer activity and a government cover-up of alien visits to Earth. Detailed descriptions of the alien craft, right down to the lights, sounds, and shockwaves. He even had the correct locations.

"How is this possible?" asked Edwards. "He can't have been talking to our people."

"I agree. Our recruiting standards are fierce. Everybody in the program is stubbornly dedicated." The general spread out copies of Criswell's birth records, school transcripts, and business filings. "He's got no criminal history. Nothing shady. He says his predictions are based on research. Exhaustive research in books and the popular press. He bundles up the ideas he finds there, and those ideas direct him to this vision of the future."

The general stubbed out his Kent. "He also claims to have sworn statements from people who have encountered the saucers."

"What people?" asked Edwards. "Where does he find them?"

"Just about every person working at Vandenburg is a civilian," said Roberts. "But I don't think any of them are talking. Even if they did talk, who can understand what they're saying?"

"That's the truth. Those slide-rule types speak a language all their own."

"Maybe it's from saucer encounters we aren't aware of. Places where we had no presence."

"Could be," said Edwards. "We've been so careful with our witnesses."

Roberts tossed a newspaper to Edwards. "Here's his column from this morning," he said. "'Saucers seen over Hollywood. Flying saucers seen over Washington D.C.' This all matches up to our reports."

Edwards scanned through the article. Peppered through the hogwash there were bits of accurate data. The closing made him chuckle. "What about this part at the end?" he said, then read aloud. "'Can your heart stand the shocking facts about grave robbers from outer space?' That's monster movie stuff. His credibility flies out the window."

"I'd have to agree, but he claims to have witness testimonials."

"Do people take this guy for real?"

"I'm sure some do," said Roberts. "He goes on talk shows and things like that, but the hosts get laughs with him. Criswell looks like he's in on the joke."

"I wonder if he knows how close to the truth he is."

"If you make a million guesses, some are bound to be right. Keep in mind, he also said all the steel and concrete in Denver will turn into a thick gel. The citizens who don't sink in the sidewalks will get trapped in the softened buildings. Many will die and the city is doomed."

"Let's hope he's wrong about that one. I want to retire there." Edwards handed the paper back to the general. "This can't be the only reason I'm here. To talk about some TV personality."

"You're right." The general set the Criswell file aside. "There is one other thing. You've seen our communication array? The tall machine in the Mojave?"

"Is it a pole supporting spinning gadgets?"

"The very one. We've been using it to attempt contact."

"Contact? How?" asked Edwards.

"We've received messages from them over radio frequencies, broadcast from their craft while they hover. For the longest time, all we could make of it was a lot of jumbled noise."

"And now, Sir?"

"We've developed a language computer," said Roberts. "A machine that breaks down and processes words the same way a mainframe works with numbers."

"Remarkable."

"They've only just got it working," said Roberts. "You witnessed our final test. One of their messages told us they'd be hovering over that spot at Camp Riley, or whatever they're calling it, at exactly the time you arrived. And there they were. We sent a message back to them with our array."

"My God, we can understand each other."

"The aliens have their own version of a language computer, and it's likely far more advanced than the one we have. Ours took ages to crack these audio bursts." The general walked to a cabinet on the far side of the room. "Turns out, the messages they sent contained over 6,000 Earth languages. All spoken at the same time, all dubbed over each other, all at a slightly different pitch."

"No wonder it sounded like a bunch of noise."

"Our language computer finally isolated the different pitches and sorted out the English one. They've got the French, Hindi, and a few hundred others isolated as well. The rest will come in time."

"General," said Edwards, "what's this all got to do with me?"

Roberts opened the cabinet. Inside a large reel-to-reel tape machine sat ready. "Well, you've been in charge of Saucer Field Activities for a long while. I think you should hear what they have to say. Do you mind?"

"Mind?" The colonel couldn't help but grin. "I'm anxious!"

"Remember, it's an approximation. They are using one machine; we are using another. Translating a translation. It may have added an adjective or a little inflection the speaker didn't intend."

The machine powered up as the general punched and toggled the controls. The reels turned, and a deep voice filled the room.

"This is Eros," it said. "A space soldier from a planet of your galaxy. Since the beginning of your time, we have been far beyond your planet. It has taken you centuries to even grasp what we developed eons of your years ago. Do you still believe it impossible we exist? You didn't actually think you were the only inhabited planet in the universe. How can any race be so stupid? Permit me to set your mind at ease. We do not want to conquer your planet. Only save it. We could have destroyed it long ago if that had been our aim."

Colonel Edwards raised his hand, and Roberts stopped the machine.

"Did you miss something?" asked the general. "I can back it up."

"No, I just have to make certain I understand what I'm hearing. Did he just say they want to *help us?*"

"Yes," said the general. "And they think we're stupid. Listen, there's more." The reels turned and the voice continued.

"Our principal purpose is friendly. I admit, we have had to take certain means which you might refer to as criminal. Once you fired your big guns at our representatives, you left us few options. Please, hear us. We only wish to help you, to warn you. With your juvenile minds, you have developed weapons and technology faster than your ability to understand what you are doing. You are on the verge of destroying the entire universe. We are part of that universe. If you persist in denying us, then we must only accept that you do not want our help. That you are unwilling to change your path. We then have no alternative but to destroy you before you destroy us. This is our last -"

"It cuts out there," said Roberts, powering down the machine. "Atmospheric conditions sometimes interfere with the transmissions."

"How many of these recordings do you have, General?"

"An even dozen up to now. We received this one over a month ago, but we didn't understand it, not until this week." Roberts moved to a map of the United States, taped to the wall. Edwards joined him there.

"Do you think they mean business?" he asked.

"We can't afford to take any chances," said Roberts. "See the pins in this map?"

"I'm guessing the red ones are live fire incidents. Breverton, Cumberland, and the like."

"Yes. Tan pins represent unconfirmed sightings. Blue are confirmed." The general tapped a blue pin in Southern California. "Tell me, Colonel, you ever been to Hollywood?"

"Years ago," said Edwards.

"You're going to be there in the morning," he walked Edwards back toward the desk and pulled a parcel out of one of the drawers. "You'll have a short meeting at the television station that carries this Criswell fellow."

"All right." Edwards knew there had to be more.

"The station is owned by Copley Press. Their newspapers have been a front for CIA operations going back to the forties, and the agency has said we can count on them to help us." The general handed the parcel to Edwards. Plain brown wrapping around what felt like a flash folder. "We can't risk communications through the regular channels, so I'm asking you to hand-deliver this to James Copley. He runs the place. Hopefully, he can get Criswell on a short leash, and maybe clue us in on his sources. Sorry to make you the bagman."

Edwards placed the parcel in his attaché case. "So, I'm on a courier mission?"

"It's much more than that. Hollywood is just one stop on this trip," said the general. "From there, you'll head about twenty miles north to the town of San Fernando. Reports have come in of saucers flying so low the shockwaves have knocked people to the ground. And there have even been stated claims of saucer landings."

"Landings? This is credible?"

"The local police have verified it. You'll be coordinating with them. The man in charge is Lieutenant Jonathon Harper. He's putting together a small group of officers to work with us. We've checked him out. He's a good egg."

"Coordinating, eh?" said Edwards. "I'll have to let them know some things."

"That's up to your discretion. This may be our best opportunity to make actual contact, eye-to-eye." Roberts handed Edwards another sheaf of orders for his attaché case and walked him to the door. "This trip is different, Colonel," he said, putting a hand on Edwards shoulder. "It isn't about saucers anymore. It's about the beings inside."

"Understood, Sir," said Edwards.

"Find them," said Roberts. "Find them and see what in hell they want."

TEN

The Plan is Far From Successful

From her station in the repair bay, Tanna signaled the control deck. Eros voice came over the speaker. "What is it, Tanna?" he said.

"Just making certain you are aware," she said, "we'll be out of the space lanes in 80 millicycles."

"Thank you, Tanna. The message from our beacon will have reached the Ruler by now."

All three saucers would arrive at Space Station Seven shortly. Tanna thought the decision to travel there was rash, but solar flare activity prevented communication with the station from Earth. It was impossible to predict how long the conditions might last and Eros refused to wait.

He launched a hyper-speed beacon carrying a message for the Ruler and led his ships into the space lanes, bound for the station. Contact was impossible at these speeds as well, but once they arrived Eros could speak to Ruler face-to-face.

"I'll acquire our docking instructions once we've cleared the lanes," she said. "In the meantime, I'm running maintenance protocols on the hand controls for our reanimated subjects." A task to keep her busy, keep her focused on something other than Eros' erratic behavior. "The controls need tuning," she said. "And if any new components are necessary, we can acquire them at Space Station Seven."

"A fine plan, Tanna," said Eros. "We'll be using those devices fiercely as we enter our next phase of preparation for Plan 9."

* * *

Once again, a message from Eros sent all of Ganymede's careful scheduling into chaos. A beacon, of all things. Eros used a beacon to announce when his ships were arriving. And he requested another audience with the Ruler.

A brusque, recorded message. Presumptive. Yet, his Excellency agreed to see Eros. In fact, he insisted on it. Ganymede had to ask why.

He found an appropriate moment during the Ruler's morning briefing. "The calendar revisions are complete, Excellency," he said. "Your time with Eros is on your schedule. But I wonder how he bypasses protocols so easily. I'm not aware of any privileges granted him above his rank. If there are any, I'd like to know, so I can better anticipate your needs."

"*Privileges above his rank,*" echoed the Ruler. "Oh Ganymede, your measured vitriol always delights me. There is no favoritism here. Eros is simply a commander pressing for a successful mission. I do not believe ambition plays a role. He wants to achieve greatness for our planet, not for himself."

The Ruler walked to the viewport wall opposite his desk, taking in the stars. "And to be absolutely clear, I planned on summoning Eros and all of his ships here for new orders. Their voluntary arrival makes that task simpler." For Ganymede, this information brought relief. He knew the Ruler wasn't one to be manipulated by an underling, and now he had an explanation.

"Going forward," said the Ruler, "affairs on Earth won't take time away from your other duties. Move it to the lowest rung, the least of your priorities."

* * *

Once more, Ganymede led Eros and Tanna into the Ruler's great chamber offices on Space Station Seven. They struck the cross-armed salutes with precision, and Ganymede returned to the adjacent antechamber.

The Ruler sat behind his desk; his expression closed. Eros paid no mind.

"We are ready to report, Excellency," he said.

"You are late," said the Ruler, searching through papers and tablets. "By many full cycles, you are late." Tanna stayed in place. Best to let her commander and his superior work this out.

"It was unavoidable," said Eros. "We attempted transmission, but solar conditions made it impossible."

"You should have transmitted as soon as conditions permitted," said the Ruler. He'd found the tablet with a transcript of Eros' message from the beacon. He reviewed it, rather than making eye contact with its creator.

"Spotty transmissions might lead to a frustrating process of inferior messaging. This dialogue is important," said Eros. "Our ships have been viewed near the scene of operations."

"Yes. There is much to discuss." The Ruler set the tablet on his desk and, for the first time since they entered the chamber, he looked at Eros. "Have *any* gains been made?"

"There are many successes, Excellency," said Eros. "We have risen three of the dead ones. Our earliest subjects remain viable, proving our methods of reanimation can be sustained over long periods. They show optimum performance on all levels. And our latest subject, a recent decedent, has exceeded those standards."

"This much is encouraging." The leader toggled his televisor. "Ganymede, a moment please."

In almost the same instant the televisor clicked off, Ganymede came through the curtains, stood tall, and crossed his arms over his chest. "Yes, Excellency?"

"I'll require a bit of your time," said the Ruler. His gaze

returned to Eros. "I wish to see one of your subjects. Ganymede will give you access to my conveyolator so you may bring it here directly, rather than parading it through the halls."

"It will be done," said Eros. He spun around to Tanna and gave her instructions in a soft voice. "Bring the big one. Our newest subject."

Tanna stepped close and spoke quietly. "Eros, the hand controllers … I've only just reassembled them. They need tuning. Calibration."

"I am aware." The edge returned to his voice. Abrupt and impatient. "All we need is ambulation, a single function. Surely you can manage to get that working."

Of course, she could. But using a raw device to bring their largest, least analyzed subject in proximity to the Ruler carried risks. Eros wasn't himself. This cruel tone. These hurried orders. And Tanna had no choice but to follow them.

She saluted. "It will be done," she said, and Ganymede led her out of the chamber.

The Ruler waited for the curtains to settle. "It is good we have a few moments, just you and I, Eros."

"Yes, Excellency?"

"I need to know you are focused on the task at hand," said the Ruler. He stood and walked Eros to the viewport. "Your mission on Earth will save all we see out there."

"I am resolute," said Eros.

"Yet, there have been missteps of late," said the Ruler. "It has come to my attention the Dictial Robotery failed to carry our message efficiently. A miscalculation of the languages."

"It is true," said Eros. "The Earth people had to develop their own system to understand our messages. Perhaps now, they will respond. Failing that, Plan 9 will have to go into action."

"And valuable time has been lost," said the Ruler. "Another thing, I've only recently received a report mentioning a city destroyed. What can you tell me about this?"

"An inaccurate statement, Excellency," said Eros. "A small

stand of dwellings and a mineral dig were demolished. One hundred such sites could fit into this space station. That is hardly a 'city.'"

"I see. Do you believe this level of damage necessary?"

"It was a lone saucer on a scout mission. The Earth military used a projectile weapon we hadn't encountered before. They managed to chip the saucer's hull. The crew did not ask for guidance. They responded by returning fire."

"One of our saucers sustained damage? From an Earth weapon?"

"A handful of fragments from the superstructure," said Eros. "Insignificant. And the Earth people have not used those projectiles since."

"Well, that shows some level of intelligence, I suppose." The Ruler returned to his desk and pushed a tablet forward. "These are new orders," he said. "Your other pilots and crews are receiving them as we speak. I have taken two ships from your command."

Eros reviewed the tablet. "But ... that will leave only my ship."

"It is necessary for you continue your mission alone," said the Ruler. "I have need of your other ships elsewhere. Even though you have risen three of the Earth dead, the plan is far from successful, and you Eros, must prove it an operational success before more time, energy, ships, and your countrymen may be spent on it."

"Excellency," said Eros, "I took this mission at your insistence. Your own science ward confirmed the Earth people are nearing the discovery of solaronite. Considering how careless they are with their atomic weapons, they may have stumbled on to it already."

"Yes. They will have access to solaronite," said the Ruler. "This is inevitable. But whether or not they discover how to *weaponize* the solaronite is a second level of conjecture. It is certainly better to deal with them now when their choices are limited. They must either acquiesce to our demands or be destroyed. They haven't the resources to negotiate. They haven't the weaponry to defend themselves."

"Yet, my mission is no longer a priority?"

"Earth is *your* highest priority," said the Ruler. "Keeping the upstarts in the Epsilon system under control is *my* highest priority, and it is why I need your other ships. The matter is closed."

The curtains parted, and Ganymede let the hulking form of what was once Inspector Daniel Clay move into the chamber. Tanna followed, manipulating a hand controller.

Ganymede returned to the conveyolator. A dead thing had been inside it and he felt the need to give it a good blast of cleanzinite.

"My word," said the Ruler. "it's enormous. No need to salute, Tanna. I can see your hands are full." As much as he wanted to keep his dour expression going, the Ruler couldn't hide his smile.

Clay's staring, off-center eyes had no color. Whites with pinpoint pupils. Tanna worked the controller and his uneven gaze locked on Eros.

"Stop him there, Tanna," said Eros, chuckling. "He's close enough."

Tanna pressed the buttons for *halt*, but the ghoul kept advancing. It raised its arms.

"Tanna, stop him," said Eros. He found himself in a corner with no way around the brute's mass. "He's hunting, Tanna. Make him halt!"

"There's a malfunction," said Tanna, mashing buttons. "The device is in contact, but it's not controlling the subject."

The ghoul's hands found Eros' neck and squeezed. "No!" hissed Eros.

"Interrupt the signal," said the Ruler. "Smash the device! Break contact altogether!"

Tanna raised the device over her head and threw it to the floor. Sparks popped under the housing, then the operating lights went dark. The ghoul released Eros and shifted to its neutral state, standing erect and looking ahead.

Eros moved out of the corner and recovered. "That was too close," he said.

Tanna picked up the controller and looked it over. "We'll need to acquire another one of these before we leave," she said.

"Yes," said the Ruler, toggling the televisor. "Ganymede, please have one of our engineers bring a decedent hand controller for Tanna."

"It will be done," answered Ganymede.

The Ruler switched off the televisor and approached the dead man standing on the other side of the chamber. "In the meantime, let's have a better look at this subject of yours."

He walked a slow circle around the remains of Inspector Clay. "Yes, he's a fine specimen. Balance is well calibrated. He stands steady and tall. Eyes open, a convincing illusion of cognizance. It's excellent work, Eros."

"Thank you, excellency, but Tanna is the one who set these tolerances."

"I used the standard protocols," said Tanna. "I merely followed the procedures."

"Following procedures, minding protocols," the Ruler looked to Eros. "Sadly, these are becoming rare traits." The Ruler returned to his desk.

"Tell me," he said, "are they all this powerful on planet Earth?"

"This one is an exception, Excellency," said Eros.

"What are your other two like?"

"One is a woman," said Tanna. "The other is an old man."

Once again, the curtains parted, and Ganymede hurried into the room. "Forgive the interruption, I have the device." He passed the hand controller to Tanna.

"Thank you," said the Ruler. "Tanna, will this serve?"

She adjusted the frequency on the controller and put Clay

through some basic moves. "Yes, Excellency," said Tanna. "It's working perfectly."

"Good," said the Ruler. "Time to take our large friend here back to your ship. Ganymede, I keep pulling you into this, but I promise this will be the last task. Please escort Tanna and her charge to the conveyolator."

"It will be done," said Ganymede. He held the curtains as Tanna guided Clay out of the chamber, then he followed them out.

The Ruler turned to Eros. "Did she say one of your subjects was an old man?"

"Yes, Excellency."

"Now that I've seen one of these Earth dead in motion, I believe I have a plan. The old man, is he the weakest of your lot?"

"Of the three, yes," said Eros.

"The old one must be sacrificed," said the Ruler, pacing the room. "You will use him to give those who have witnessed your work a reason to stay away. You will shock their minds."

"And how shall I go about this 'mind-shock?'"

"Re-land on Earth, the same location as before," said the Ruler. "Send the old one to enter the same dwelling as before. Wait for him to be in full view of the residents, then cut off the control circuits and cycle your ship's decomposer ray."

"With a subject this long deceased, the flesh will disintegrate," said Eros. "There will be nothing but bones and a shroud."

"Precisely. The result will astound those watching," said the Ruler. "These are primitive people. The display will likely cause them to flee. Even if they have the wherewithal to report this fantastic sight, they won't be believed. You'll gain time, Eros. Time to acquire other recruits from the cemetery, then establish a new scene of operations elsewhere."

"Yes, Excellency," said Eros, saluting. "It will be done."

"Report to me when this has been accomplished." The Ruler looked to the stars through the viewport again. "Eros," he said, "the

Earth people are getting closer to that which we fear. Since they will not listen or respect our existence, they cannot help but believe our powers when they see their own dead walking around again, brought about by our advancement in such things. As soon as you have enough of the dead recruits, march them on the capitals of the Earth, let nothing stand in your way. Their own dead will be used to make them accept our existence, and believe in that fact."

ELEVEN

Grave Robbers from Outer Space

In California, Edwards had access to comforts he hadn't seen in months. Instead of a driver, they gave him his own car. A Chevy Bel Air, brand new from a rental agency. Much nicer than a dusty jeep.

He had a room, too. A real room at the Lazy Acres Motel all to himself with a full bed and a bathroom. No billeting at a far-off base this time. They wanted him rested and free to move about.

And take care of business. Check things off the list. Work the problem, find the solution, and end this thing once and for all.

First up, a meeting at the KCOP Channel 13 Studios in Hollywood. It didn't take long. James Copley, head of the company and puppet for the CIA, was surprised anyone took Criswell seriously. He offered to cancel the show. Edwards said it was better to keep him broadcasting but supervise his copy. The government needed crackpots. It helped to discredit certain theories. That made the Amazing Criswell useful, as long as he backed off his claims about government conspiracies and flying saucers.

Next came a long ride along most of Mulholland Drive, offering the colonel wonderful views of the wide-open spaces making up most of Los Angeles, and the thick layer of smog covering them. His destination was the Nike Missile Site at San

Vicente Mountain, a last-minute addition to his itinerary. Edwards wondered how many people in the valleys below knew they were surrounded by sixteen such missile stations.

Around the Pentagon, officials outside the Initiative were always looking to debunk saucer sightings. They had a new theory - local missile battalions testing their launch systems created lights and sounds the public mistook for alien craft.

General Roberts needed to squash this theory, as it stole focus from the actual situation. Edwards got tasked with getting straight answers from the source.

His meeting with Major Kyle Jarvis of the Air Defense Unit eighty-sixed the theory quickly. "They call our missile sites 'The Ring of Supersonic Steel,'" he said. "Leave it to the military, right? Sounds like this is something out of *Space Patrol*. But look around. They should have called it 'The Ring of Concrete and Coyotes.'" Edwards agreed. Chain link. Single-story, plain buildings. The missiles and their launchers lay hidden underground. Most of the establishment looked like a big slab.

"When the launchers get tested," said Edwards, "can a civilian on the ground or in an airplane see lights or a glow? Maybe hear systems powering up?"

"Impossible," said Jarvis. "We don't do test fires, we're too close to the city. That's the directive, no launches from these sites without a target, and that's never happened. Most of our business is running active radar, looking for a Tupolev. The drills and tests are just to make sure the racks come out of their holes and line up the way we want. It's not loud, you can't hear it past the fence line. And we don't have anything in the air."

As the men parted company, Jarvis added, "It's a shame our Chatsworth station isn't up and running yet. Their radar could pinpoint your San Fernando space birds in a hot second."

With his morning meetings complete and successful, Edwards had time for another rare indulgence - lunch. At a restaurant. With a newspaper.

He had a bowl of beans and spaghetti at a place in Burbank

called Chili John's. He sat at the big, U-shaped counter and read the *Los Angeles Times*. The biggest article went on and on about petitions against a new business tax.

People worried about City Hall and their wallets, unaware of the hostile force from the stars watching their planet. The chili was terrific, but this lunch didn't relax him. He heard the civilians sharing jokes and stories. They didn't know the world may be torn out from under them at any moment.

He pictured the beam from Breverton slicing Chili John's in two, then torching Burbank off the map. It solidified Edwards' resolve. He had to find the aliens.

* * *

The saucer entered Earth's solar system, passing the outer rim of small planetoids. Tanna had the hand controls functioning perfectly and each of the dead stood ready.

Eros reviewed an audio parcel via the Dictial Robotery over and over again.

"What is it, Eros?" asked Tanna. "Are these new messages for the Earth people?"

"No. One of our other ships received this audio burst on our last visit," said Eros. "They weren't sure what to make of it, so they passed it to me just before we left Space Station Seven.

"It is a message, but it's not for the Earth People," said Eros. "It is *from* them."

"A response?"

"Yes - after all this time."

"This could change everything," said Tanna. "What do they say?"

"As with all matters involving the Earth people, their intention is unclear. They are aware of our operations at the cemetery. They are sending 'a soldier called Edwards' there to meet us."

"A soldier? Are you sure?"

"Yes, if we can trust the translation. And if they are sending a soldier, I can't imagine their aim is a peaceful dialogue."

* * *

It didn't take long to get from Burbank to the San Fernando Police Station. The colonel was introduced first to Lieutenant Harper, then to Officers Kelton, Greene, and Tucker. The lieutenant had kept the team small, just as he'd been instructed. A good sign.

Edwards had a briefing with Harper, alone, over mugs of coffee in the interrogation room. It started with Harper walking the colonel through the events of the last few months. Maps, case files, and photographs covered the table.

"That's when it started," said Harper. "Lights in the sky, strange winds, crazy sounds. But sometimes you get odd reports like that, you know? People get rattled by something they read in the papers or saw on TV. Then, when it's late and quiet, they start seeing things."

"I can imagine how that happens," said Edwards, "but are you saying all of this is some mass hallucination?"

"Far from it," said Harper. "I thought so at first, but along with those lights and sounds came something very real, a double murder. Two people torn to pieces and hidden away in the Briar Glade Cemetery. It's this green area on the map."

"Big property."

"That's why it took a long time for someone to stumble across the bodies," said Harper. "The night they were discovered we went to the graveyard to investigate. And our commander, Inspector Daniel Clay, he got attacked and killed the same way."

"How did it happen?" asked Edwards.

"He went off on his own to look for clues. The other murders happened at least a week before. More than a week before, that's what the coroner said. After so much time, we didn't think we'd find anything helpful. But Clay found the killers."

"No sign of them? His assailants?"

"Nothing. No physical evidence, either. And that same night, just before Clay fell, those intense lights filled the sky. The wind and noise, too. All around the cemetery."

"You have witnesses?"

"Me, for one," said Harper. "That's why your people didn't have to spend much time convincing me about alien spacecraft. I got knocked over by the exhaust from one of those things. Blinded me and rattled by eardrums."

"Is that the only time you had an encounter?"

"No, once more. Just a few nights ago."

Edwards flipped a few pages in his report, following the timeline. "That was when a woman was attacked."

"Yes," said Harper, handing the colonel a file. "A lady alone while her husband was off on business. An intruder forced a door and got into her home. Tried to grab her, then chased her all over the cemetery. A good Samaritan in a passing car spotted her, picked her up, and brought her here, to the police station."

"Lucky for her. She might have ended up like those others, like your commander."

"Exactly. We headed over to investigate and there we were in that damn graveyard again. Trying to find this intruder or footprints or any other clues, and we hear the exact same sound. No lights this time, but the same rumbling sound. A saucer, I'm sure of it. Then, a little later, we came across this grave that's been busted into. It's all dug up and the body's gone missing. Still missing. Worse yet, it's the grave of Inspector Clay, our commander. Don't that beat all?"

"This woman, the one who got chased through the graveyard, is she all right?"

"Yes. Minor cuts and bruises. She had to stay at the hospital overnight for shock, but she's fine now. Trent, Paula Trent is her name. Husband is Jeff Trent, pilot for American Airlines."

Jeff Trent. His name appeared more than once in Edwards' files. He witnessed a pair of saucer encounters, once from a plane and again at his home. Now this intruder appears at the same home. And there were more sightings, murders, and a missing corpse right over his fence in the cemetery.

"If we can," said Edwards, "I'd like to talk to the Trents."

"I'll have one of my officers set it up," said Harper. He paced around the room. "Look, Colonel Edwards, I'm a cop. Have been for decades. Cut my teeth in Philly and came out here for some peace and quiet. Case like this, well, you try to look past all the comic-strip malarky and find the facts. There has to be something you can prove, something you can know. From there, you can build a picture, an image of what's really happening. But this case? Nothing. No connections. Nothing but suspicions and theories, and nothing to hang a fact on.

"Facts. Shocking facts ... about grave robbers from outer space."

"How's that, Colonel?"

"Just something I heard."

* * *

As Jupiter moved over the observation dome, Eros rehearsed his future dialogue with the soldier. Sorted all his possible points and responses. Did the Ruler know about the message from Earth? Was this the reason he sent Eros off without the rest of his ships?

Long ago, on Ardavia, Eros led the coalition that successfully negotiated peace. The Ardavians saw reason, appreciated the wisdom from a more mature planet, and ceased solaronite production.

The following year, across the galaxy on the planet Verkassis, the results were tragic. Negotiations broke down. The Verkassians believed Eros had a hidden agenda. They thought this visiting alien wanted to trick them into falling behind in an interstellar arms race. Try as he may, Eros failed to make them see reason.

The Verkassians accelerated their weapons programs. They refined larger and larger quantities of solaronite. The Ruler had no other choice. He sent an armada and they rained beam weapons on Verkassis until the entire surface became cinders.

Will this Earth soldier understand the dire stakes? Will he be able to articulate the warning to his superiors? And will they listen? Eros anticipated a delicate situation. He couldn't even rely on his carefully chosen words. The Dictial Robotery might mangle them.

* * *

When Kelton called to see if they'd be willing to talk with the colonel, the Trents jumped at the chance. They were desperate for help with the extraordinary turns their lives had taken.

So, a few hours after Edwards' arrival at the police station, Kelton drove Harper and the colonel to the Trent's house. He stayed with the patrol vehicle next to the carport while his superiors joined the couple on their patio.

Paula had set out some bottles of pop and a few snacks.

"Mr. and Mrs. Trent ... this is Colonel Edwards from Washington, D.C." said Lieutenant Harper. They exchanged greetings and introductions all around. "The colonel would like to ask you a few questions."

"Questions? What about, Colonel?" asked Jeff.

Still standing, the colonel motioned toward a chair. "May I sit down?"

"Oh, I'm sorry," said Paula, laughing. "Please do. Everyone, take a seat."

Edwards pulled the notebook from his attaché case. "I want to ask you about your strange experiences," he said. "Let's start with the night you saw something fly over the house."

* * *

Behind the knoll in Briar Glade Cemetery, the saucer landed in shadow mode: No lights, no sound, no wind. Unless you were standing underneath the vessel, you'd have no idea they'd arrived.

Tanna activated the vid-points. They saw every approach on the televisor. They had the upper hand.

* * *

Edwards had filled nine pages of his notebook with hand-coded entries. He did his best to maintain a stone face, but the description of Paula Trent's attacker had him rattled. "Sorry to make you go through all this again, Mrs. Trent," he said.

"It's all right," said Paula. Jeff stood behind her, his hand on her shoulder. "That's the end of the story, anyway. I woke up at the hospital the next morning. The police brought me home and it's been quiet here since then. I hope I never see such a sight again."

"Well after your description I don't think I'd want to see it either," said Edwards. He paged back through his notes. "Oh, one thing more … after you were forced to the ground by that blast of wind, was it a hot or cold blast?"

The Trents shared a look. Both wondered why such a thing mattered. "It's kind of hard to explain," said Jeff. "Not hot, not cold, just a terrific force. We couldn't get off the ground."

"The light blinded me so badly I couldn't see a thing," said Paula. "We felt the pressure of the wind, it held us in place. When the glare left us, I saw a glowing ball disappearing off in the distance."

"Which way?" asked the colonel.

She pointed toward the edge of Briar Glade, just past Kelton and the patrol car. "Over there," she said, "toward the cemetery."

* * *

Eros and Tanna watched Paula and the others on the televisor. "It's like she's pointing right at us," said Tanna. She highlighted individuals on the screen. "We've seen these people before. This one and the one in uniform by the car, they are both police officers if I remember correctly."

"Yes," said Eros. "Enforcing local Earth laws. And those two, the man and woman, they live in the dwelling." He expanded the image on Colonel Edwards. "But we haven't seen this one – he hasn't been here before. The uniform is different from those worn by the police officers. He must be the soldier spoken of in the message, the one called 'Edwards.'"

"What is our next action, Eros?"

"We will follow the Ruler's plan. Use the old man to clear the area."

"It will be done," said Tanna, toggling controls on her console. "The soldier will likely remain. Follow his orders and come looking for us."

"I will welcome that," said Eros.

The outside hatch slipped open, and the old man's reanimated corpse left the saucer. As before, it trod through the graveyard toward the Trent home. Its stasis matrix had been disabled. Decomposition had begun.

* * *

The colonel tucked the notebook into his attaché case. "This is the most fantastic story I've ever heard," he said.

"And every word of it's true, too," said Jeff.

"That's the fantastic part of it," said Edwards. He looked skyward. "Well, we must have been talking a long time. It's got so dark."

Paula checked her watch. "Just an hour," she said. "You're right, though. Looks like night has come early." Then, her pleasant smile disappeared. Her eyes went wide. She clutched Jeff's hand.

"What is it, Darling?" he asked. Then he felt it, too. A dizzy sensation, and he heard a faint, whirring sound.

"Hey, does anybody else hear that?" asked Harper. A quick look around the patio told him everyone heard it. And it became stronger. He hollered toward the patrol car. "You see anything out there Kelton?"

"Too dark, Lieutenant," said Kelton. "But something's started stinking awful bad. Skunk maybe?" He shook out a Pall Mall and lit it to cover the smell.

Jeff Trent held his wife close. "There's something out there," he said. He was sure of it. Everyone felt the same unsteady trepidation.

"Stop right there!" shouted Kelton. He drew his weapon and aimed toward the darkness of the graveyard. Everyone got on their feet. Harper pulled his revolver from his shoulder holster. Edwards fished his Browning Hi-Power out of the attaché case.

"Mr. and Mrs. Trent, you'd better get back," he said.

"I said stop!" hollered Kelton. "Hold it right there, or I'll shoot!" The old man ignored the young officer's request and continued his relentless advance. He moved into the light cast from the Trent's patio. A tall figure draped in black cloth.

"It's the one from the other night!" cried Paula. Jeff held her tighter and turned to put himself between his wife and the ghoul.

"There's no shot," said Edwards. "Have your man get clear."

"You're right," said Harper. He called out, "Kelton! Fall back here with us!"

"Coming," said Kelton. He split his focus between the advancing ghoul and finding a clear path to the others. He took careful, backward steps with his revolver trained on the foul thing. The smell of rot choked him. Those still eyes drilled into him.

He fired two shots into the old man's chest. And it kept coming.

The colonel and Harper stepped closer. The dead thing walked on the patio now, just ten steps from the Trents. Kelton emptied his gun as the ghoul charged him. It struck the officer's head with both fists.

As Kelton fell to the concrete, Harper and Edwards fired shot after shot. They saw their bullets tear into it, but it didn't slow down.

* * *

"Their weapons are clearly ineffective," said Tanna. "Yet, they continue using them."

"They are striking different targets on the subject," said Eros. "Some projectiles aimed at the torso, others at the head. They may be searching for a weak point."

"Perhaps," said Tanna.

"In any case, it is time for the last step in the Ruler's plan." With that, Eros engaged the decomposer ray.

* * *

"I'm empty," said Harper. He turned the revolver in his hand, ready to pistol-whip the ghoul.

"Me too," said Edwards as he fired his last shot.

For a moment, the whirring sound changed to a static buzz. Then silence. The ghoul dropped to the ground and curled up, covered completely under its shroud.

Whatever lay beneath the cloth held resolutely still. Harper and Edwards shared a look.

The lieutenant reloaded his gun, then leveled it at the shape. With a nod, Edwards moved toward the shroud's ragged edge, flinching when he got hold of it. Both men held their breath, and as Edwards threw back the rancid covering, Harper leaned in.

There was no need to fire. The object of their fear had somehow become a skinless heap of bones. Paula Trent felt sick. The men felt angry.

"What do you make of that?" asked Edwards.

"You got me," said Harper. "It didn't look that way a minute ago. Are you all right, Mr. and Mrs. Trent?"

"Never thought I'd be so happy to see a skeleton," said Paula.

"Yeah," said Jeff. "Somehow, this feels safer."

"What about your man?" asked Edwards.

"Oh, that's right!" The lieutenant checked on his officer, tapped his hands. "Hey Kelton, you there? You really got your bell rung." His color looked good, and his hands were warm.

Kelton's eyes fluttered open, then went wide. "Did you see that thing? Did you get it?"

The lieutenant shared a smile with Edwards and said, "He's all right."

"Where is it?" asked Kelton.

"We got it," said Harper.

"It didn't fall, and I fired every bullet I had."

"So did we," said Harper. "I don't know what it was or what happened, but unless that stack of bones can reassemble itself, it's out of the running now."

TWELVE

Toward the Cemetery

"The decomposition is complete," said Tanna. "No flesh material remains on the old man." She shut down the decomposer station. "There's nothing left but the wrappings and brittle bone."

Eros watched the scene unfold on the Trent's patio. "As we theorized," he said. "Yet, the Earth people are not fearful. They showed more concern before we engaged the decomposer ray."

"Indeed," said Tanna. "They do not flee. Instead, they show relief at the subject's conversion to skeletal remains. As if the dead one is no longer a threat to them."

The Ruler's plan had failed.

* * *

"Have you seen anything like this before, Colonel?" asked Paula. She and the others sat in a group of patio chairs Jeff had positioned away from the bones.

"No, nothing like this," said Edwards. "Saucers are the limit of my experience."

"So, this is something new," said Harper. "Are you sure it was the same one from the other night, Mrs. Trent?"

"Of course," said Paula, taking Jeff's hand. "You think I'd forget a thing like that?"

"You know, honey, I'm thinking something crazy, but I've got to mention it," said Jeff. "Did you get a look at its face?"

Paula lit a cigarette. As soon as they saw her reach for the pack, Harper and Kelton did the same. "Looked like the man from the real estate office," she said.

"Yeah," said Jeff, nodding.

"Hang on," said Edwards. "Are you saying you recognized it? Someone you knew?"

"There's this fellow who owned North Valley Realty," said Jeff. "His wife worked there too. She was our agent, sold us this place. We saw her all the time. We only met the old man once. Just a handshake on the day we signed the paperwork for the house. But yeah, it looked like him."

"Wait a minute … he died weeks ago," said Harper. "He's in a vault right over the fence there at Briar Glade. His service was on the day Inspector Clay was attacked."

"I know," said Paula. "It's impossible."

"After all I've seen," said Edwards, "I can't say what is or isn't possible. Our best bet is to head over to the cemetery and see what we can find." With that, the men stood.

Paula stubbed out her cigarette and stood up as well. "I'm certainly not staying here alone," she said. "What if there's more of those things running around?"

"It's probably best if every one of us comes along," said Edwards. "We'll stay together, be careful."

"Makes sense," said Harper. "We can all fit in the patrol car. Kelton, are you feeling all right?"

"Yes, Lieutenant. I'm much better now." He took a deep breath and rubbed his neck, then looked at the heap of bones. "Say, if those are human remains, isn't this a crime scene?"

The group puzzled on this for a moment. "What do you think, Colonel Edwards?" asked Harper.

"Your officer is correct," he said. "But please say they were found where they are right now. No sense letting anyone know a skeleton walked here under its own power."

"You heard the man, Kelton," said Harper. "Go to the car, get on the blower, and have Greene come down here to take charge. He can coordinate with the coroner and the morgue wagon."

"Yes, Lieutenant." Kelton ran toward the car. Harper called after him.

"And I want hazard protocols," he said. "Like it's an unknown chemical. Breathers, coveralls, you know what I mean. This thing might have space bugs."

"Come to think of it," said Edwards, "I touched that cloak, or whatever it is. May I use your washroom, Mr. and Mrs. Trent?"

"Oh please, feel free," said Paula. "Just past the kitchen, first on the right. Can't miss it."

"Thank you. After that, I may need to use your phone."

"There's one in the spare room," said Jeff. "End of the same hall. It's got a door if you need privacy."

"I'm sure I will."

* * *

"They are coming here," said Eros. "And once they are near this location, I think we should send power to the field generators. Make the ship glow."

"Lure them here?" said Tanna. "A bold idea, Eros."

"The Ruler underestimated their resolve." He highlighted the image of the colonel on the televisor. "If this soldier, Edwards, wishes to have a dialogue, I will not deny him. We will speak here, on this deck. Seeing our capabilities may help him understand our position."

For the first time in many cycles, Tanna saw the Eros she once knew. The one she wanted to learn from all those years ago when she joined the service. A conversation between planetary representatives was the only hope they had for a peaceful resolution, and it would happen soon.

* * *

Kelton parked the patrol car on the far path, well inside Briar Glade. Tomorrow morning, when all this was over, he'd send another anonymous letter to the Amazing Criswell. These things shouldn't be kept secret.

Everyone stepped out and clocked the area around the car. Lieutenant Harper moved to the trunk and passed around flashlights. "Colonel," he said, "I've been out here so often you'd think I'd taken a lease on this place."

The colonel tracked along the headstones with his flashlight. "Not a long lease, I hope."

"I see what you mean," said Harper. "But you know, I can't help but feel the answer's out here somewhere."

Away from the others, Jeff held Paula close. "There's a big moon tonight," he said. "It'll help us see. You should stay in the car."

"I want to go, too," said Paula. She walked Jeff over to the lieutenant. "We're all staying together, right?"

"Now Darling," said Jeff, "we're looking for trouble out there. If we find it, I don't want you anywhere near it."

"I'm not going to stay here alone," said Paula. "Not on your life."

"No one is saying you have to," said Harper. "Officer Kelton will stay here too, won't you Kelton?" Harper nodded firmly as he said it.

"Yes, Lieutenant," said Kelton, mirroring the nod.

"Good," said Harper. "How are you fixed for ammunition?"

"Revolver's loaded, and I've got plenty more bullets," said Kelton. The words came fast as he second-guessed his decision to guard Mrs. Trent. "But guns didn't stop the thing over at the house. Didn't even slow it down."

"Look, if there's real trouble jump in the car," said Harper. "You and Mrs. Trent get out of here. Blast the horn and the sirens on your way so we know something's up." The lieutenant pulled a map of the grounds from his coat and spread it out on the hood of the patrol car. "Colonel, come and have a look at this map."

The colonel moved next to Harper. They only just got oriented when they saw Paula and Kelton enter the front seat of the patrol car. "You'll have to show me," said Paula. "You may need to shoot while I drive."

"Okay," said Kelton. "This toggles on the lights up top. And this is the siren." He eyed the lieutenant through the windshield. "But don't hit it now."

"Modern women ..." said Harper, quietly.

"Yeah, they been that way all down through the ages," said Edwards. "Especially in a spot like this."

"Mr. Trent, please join us over here," said Harper. Jeff did a half-jog to the front of the car. "I was just showing the colonel here, these are the places where we've had unexplainable occurrences. We'll start down this path, to where the first bodies were discovered."

"All right," said Jeff.

Harper turned him away from the car. "Do you have a gun?" he asked.

"No, I don't."

"Know how to use one?"

"After four years in the Marine Corps? Absolutely," said Jeff.

"I'll get you a pistol from the trunk," said Harper.

* * *

The televisor displayed the group around the patrol car. "They carry firearms," said Tanna.

"Not all of them," said Eros. "I believe the soldier left his weapon behind. Perhaps he has a different perspective."

Tanna looked at the moon through the observation dome. "Eros, perhaps we can give them all a different perspective."

"How?"

"What if the dialogue with the Earth people happened in

orbit? Once they arrive here, we launch. They will see their own planet through the dome. The first of their kind to do so."

"This is a bold idea, Tanna."

"They will realize how small - how fragile their world is. All they have ever known, viewed in single glance. Such a vision changes you, humbles you. It may fill them with the need to protect their frail planet."

"I agree," said Eros, "but they will never come willingly. If we invite them into space, they will suspect some trickery."

"Then we won't invite them," said Tanna. "I'll set up a timed launch with a long countdown. Start it running just before they come on deck. We won't be near a control panel. The ship will simply lift off."

* * *

Edwards, Harper, and Trent moved along the graveyard walkways. First they examined the area the where grave diggers were found, then the path where Clay fell. The colonel had a lot of questions. Jeff had a lot of doubts.

"All of this," he said, "it's incredible. I'm not sure how much help I can offer."

"You've had multiple encounters, Mr. Trent," said Edwards. "The cockpit of your airplane, the flyover at your house, and tonight on your patio. You've had more contacts than any civilian I'm aware of. Having you with us is helpful."

"What do you expect we'll find here?" asked Jeff.

"There's only one answer Mr. Trent," said the lieutenant. "We'll know when we find it." Leading this grisly tour weighed on Jonathan Harper. He displayed a gruff disposition for the benefit of the others, but this business shook him up. Murders he hadn't solved. Events he had no explanations for. Briar Glade was meant to be a place for eternal rest. For Harper, it was a catalyst for anger.

"Inspector Clay's grave is right over this way," he said.

"The one you told me got broken into?" asked Edwards.

"Yes," said Harper. "Police tape is still up."

Edwards, Harper, and Trent moved along the graveyard walkways.

* * *

"It is time," said Eros. "I'm powering up the field generators now."

"The automated launch parameters are set," said Tanna. "After I turn this control, we will lift off in sixty millicycles."

"Excellent. I do hope they see reason," said Eros. "If not, they will need to be eliminated."

"Must we kill them?"

"Yes," said Eros. "They have seen too much. The soldier and the police leader are credible sources of information. Others will believe what they say. Left alive, they will inform their superiors about our mission. This could scuttle Plan 9. Unacceptable."

"I understand," said Tanna. "Let's hope the dialogue goes well. Then we won't need to kill any of them." She tapped the televisor displaying Officer Kelton and Paula Trent at the patrol vehicle. "What of the others in the car?"

"We'll need to keep them under control. Send both of our remaining dead to their location. Incapacitate the policeman. Order the big one to bring the female Earth person here. Non-lethal protocols."

Tanna powered up the reanimation console. "It will be done."

* * *

Police tape stretched between stakes at the site of Daniel Clay's grave. Pieces of his shattered coffin had been taken into evidence. The headstone hadn't moved, nor had the piles of dirt.

The lieutenant lifted the tape, allowing Edwards to duck under. "Be careful, the edge isn't stable," said Harper.

"I'll watch my step," said Edwards. He walked around the perimeter and looked into the grave with his flashlight. "This may sound unusual," he said, "but it almost looks to me like someone had broken out instead of in."

"One of my men said the same thing," said Harper. "But that's impossible, isn't it?"

"I wonder," said Jeff.

Harper wasn't having it. "Look, some things just can't happen."

"Well after the apparition we saw draped across Mr. Trent's patio, I would say we should keep our minds open to anything," said Edwards. "Even horrible, impossible things.

Earlier this evening, did a dead old man attack one of Harper's officers? He had a hard time swallowing that. Because if it was true, then the same thing might have happened to Clay. Taken away by the aliens for experiments, or Heaven knows what.

The lieutenant couldn't face that. "Look, Colonel," he said, "I'm a policeman. I've got to deal in facts."

"Here's a fact," said Jeff. "Paula and the farmer said they saw two of those things. Who knows how many more are running around out here?"

"I guess I'll have to go along with you there, Mr. Trent," said Harper. "Yeah, I can feel it. I bet my badge right now we haven't seen the last of those weirdies."

"Where to next?" asked Edwards.

"There's part of the fence line we should look at, just along -" Harper stopped talking. He saw light coming through the trees. "Do you see that?" he asked.

They did. All of them saw it. Something glowed on the other side of the knoll.

"Work crew maybe?" asked Jeff.

"Don't hear any machinery," said Edwards. "No voices, nothing."

"We've got to check it out," said Harper. "But move carefully."

* * *

With everything going on, Paula Trent thought she'd never sleep again. So much nervous energy. So many emotions ricocheted through her. She hadn't slept well since the night she first encountered the tall man in the black wrappings, now a skeleton on her patio.

But once she got settled in the back seat of the patrol car with a blanket around her shoulders, her eyes drifted closed. The area around the car was quiet. Dark. Just the crickets. The policeman, Kelton, paced around but didn't make noise.

After just fifteen minutes in the car, she fell asleep.

Wherever Kelton looked, he saw nothing. But just out of his field of view, he thought he saw movement in the shadows. He'd spin and look there. Again, nothing. And again, something off to the side. His mind playing tricks.

Kelton's head was a bad neighborhood. Things didn't go well if he spent time there. Especially at night. Especially alone. And with Mrs. Trent sleeping, he couldn't distract himself with conversation.

He tugged another Pall Mall out of the pack. As he scratched the match on the the book, an off-center pressure filled his ear, as if he'd been swimming. He tilted his head, and the pressure moved to the other side, joined by a whirring sound. Something moved just out of sight to his left. He spun.

Six steps away, a large figure lumbered toward him, arms reaching forward. Kelton's flashlight beam lit the man's face.

"My God," said Kelton. "Inspector Clay, is that you?" A deep wound marred his forehead. The corners of his mouth hung in a grimace, but this was certainly the man who's body had been missing all this time. And he kept stepping closer.

The cigarette dropped out of the young officer's mouth. "Hey Inspector, don't you know me?" he asked. "It's Kelton. Paul Kelton. Don't you remember?" One of Clay's enormous hands surrounded Kelton's shoulder. The other clamped around his throat and squeezed.

Paula woke to tapping on the car window, behind her head. It took her a moment to remember where she was. And one moment after that, she became aware of the whirring sound she'd come to dread. It meant awful things.

And the tapping got louder.

She looked out the front windshield and saw Kelton in the headlights. A huge man had him by the neck. Her eyes darted to the left, checking that the driver's side locks were down.

They were.

She reached over the seat and slapped the lock on the front passenger door. It was already down. She turned to the last lock, the door she'd been sleeping against, and discovered the source of the tapping. A woman outside hunched over with her jagged finger striking the window again and again. Trying to reach inside, trying to pull up the pin, as if she didn't understand the glass blocked her.

The woman put her face against the window and studied the pin, one eye scarred closed, the other wide and red. Finger still scratching, still trying to unlock the door. Straggles of her thin hair stuck to the glass.

Paula couldn't speak. Couldn't scream. She knew this woman once. They had lunches and drinks. And she passed away weeks ago. Still tapping, the dead thing turned its head at an unnatural angle and stared at her.

In front of the car, Kelton passed out and the ghoul let him drop. The non-lethal protocols had engaged successfully. Clay moved around the car, to the other rear door.

Paula Trent was surrounded by the dead.

Clay ripped the door off the chassis and tossed it away. Paula screamed. She scooted away from him until the back of her head pressed against the opposite window. She felt the dead woman's steady thumps on the glass but refused to look behind her.

Clay reached into the car and Paula kicked at him. His off-center, pallid eyes stared at her and away from her at the same time. His cold fingers caught her calf and wrapped around it, tight.

She fainted. Gently, he pulled her from the back seat and lifted her into his arms.

The other ghoul still tapped on the window, trying to reach the door lock. As instructed.

* * *

The men had to leave the path and move through the bramble and trees to reach the other side of the knoll. There, resting on a twenty-foot-wide metallic cylinder, stood a glowing saucer the size of Jeff Trent's house. A ship from another planet.

They crouched near a tree and whispered when they spoke. "It's just like the one I saw on the plane," said Jeff. "Except for the bottom piece. Mine just had a bowl under the saucer section."

"That's new to me as well," said Edwards. "Then again, I've never seen one on the ground. Maybe it's their landing gear." He shifted toward the ship. "I've got to move in closer."

"Not alone," said Harper. "We stick together."

"Count me in," said Jeff. "I need to know why they've been after me."

They started down the hill slowly, hunched over and sneaking. Then Edwards stood tall. "You two should know, they might be expecting me," he said.

"How's that?" asked Harper.

"My superiors have been trying to communicate with them. Find out what they're after. If the message got through, they'll know I'm here to talk with them."

Trent and Harper looked to each other and shared a smile. "Well," said Jeff, "there isn't much sense in sneaking around then."

"Absolutely right," said Harper. "Let's go knock and tell them we're here."

The three men strode to the saucer's base. They walked around it twice but couldn't find a hatchway. Only small windows at eye-level every seven feet.

Edwards rapped his knuckle against the surface, expecting to hear a clang. Instead, the sound bowed. "Never heard metal sound like that before," he said. Harper had his face pressed to one of the windows. "What do you see?" asked the colonel.

"Only my reflection. Must be some kind of one-way glass."

"So how do we get into this thing?" asked Jeff.

Harper looked up at the saucer, looming all around him. "I'm not sure I want to find out," he said.

THIRTEEN

All You of Earth are Idiots

Four different vid-points around the base of the ship showed the trio of Earth men. Eros sat close to the prime view and spoke as if they could hear him. "In just a few moments," he said, "you will be the first *living* Earth people ever to enter a celestial ship."

Tanna stood just behind him. "Do you see screen 12, Eros?" she asked. "Our large test subject is bringing the woman here. Shall I have the other dead one follow them?"

"No," said Eros. "Have her patrol the perimeter of the cemetery. We may need her at the ready if more people arrive."

"It will be done." Tanna toggled the controls on the reanimation console. The woman ceased her pawing at the car window and walked toward Briar Glade's northern fence, the start of a her rounds.

"Let's allow the others inside," said Eros. "Prime the automated launch, then open the outer hatch."

✳ ✳ ✳

The men completed another fruitless lap around the saucer's base. "It's seamless, apart from these windows" said Jeff. "I don't see a single join, let alone an entry point."

"Yes," said Edwards. "It's one piece."

"Like a big pipe," said Harper. As if that were the password, a thin, iridescent line traced an oval onto the surface in front of the lieutenant. It grew until it became a foot taller than him and twice as wide.

"Look out!" said Jeff. All three men backed away as the oval outline became a deep groove. It stopped glowing, and the shape it carved out slid away, revealing a dim, shallow hall.

"There's our door." said Edwards. He stepped toward it.

"Hang on," said Jeff. "Let's talk for a second before we go in."

"It's what we're here for," said Harper.

"I know," said Jeff, "but the way these saucers speed around we might just get in there and ZIP! Off it goes."

"It's a chance we'll have to take," said Edwards.

"I feel nervous in a regular airplane. This can't be much worse," said Harper. "Might just as well see what the inside of one of these looks like." All agreed, they'd be going in.

Trent drew his gun. "I'll tell you one thing, if a little green man jumps out at me I'm shooting first and asking questions later." He stepped through the door ahead of the others. The hall curved, like the exterior. Only a few yards were visible.

The others followed. "Doesn't feel like a trap," said Harper.

"Good ones never do," said Edwards.

The oval door slid back into place. With a flash, it's outline vanished, leaving the smooth wall behind. Edwards touched the spot. "Only one way to go now," he said. The men moved deeper into the ship.

After about twenty steps, the hall looked the same coming and going. "It feels like we're on a treadmill," said Jeff. "Like all this is moving around us."

"It is peculiar," said Edwards. "But it has to lead somewhere." The hall ended at last, emptying into circular room large enough to hold ten people.

Harper moved to the center. "There's no where else to go," he said. "Maybe another one of those trick doors will show up."

As the others joined him, the hallway entrance they'd just stepped through sealed and vanished. The floor shook, and all felt movement. "It's an elevator," said Edwards.

"To where?" asked Jeff.

* * *

"They're rising to the outer chamber now," said Eros. "The Dictial Robotery is engaged, we will be able to converse with them." He felt a pressure in his temples and chest he hadn't experienced since his academy days. Anxiety. Why did these Earth people summon such feelings? The Ruler had told him to stay objective. Success depended on it. He must maintain control.

The soldier, the one called "Edwards," he had merit. Yet, two others were about to gain access to the control deck. Still, if "Edwards" felt more at ease with these men accompanying him, they would be permitted.

"The timer for the automated launch has been engaged," said Tanna. "In sixty millicycles, we lift off and move into a class-seventeen orbit."

"Excellent," said Eros. "All is ready. Time to bring them in." He moved a lever on the wall, and the main hatch opened.

* * *

The floor stopped shaking and the circular room went still. "I guess we're here," said Edwards. An oval glow appeared in the wall and an opening appeared. Harper and Trent raised their guns.

"Put those away," said Edwards. "Don't give them anything to react to."

"You sure about that?" asked Harper.

"I'm not sure about any of this. But if someone came through my door waving a gun around, I'd get cranky."

With a nod, Harper holstered his revolver. Trent dropped his gun into his jacket pocket.

The three men stepped through the opening.

The other areas of the saucer they'd seen were featureless. Smooth walls and empty spaces. The control deck was another matter. Banks of switches and dials. Consoles and workstations with blinking lights and levers. Above their heads, a vast clear dome with an uninterrupted view of the night sky.

In the center of all of it, a man and a woman stood at what Edwards recognized as "parade rest," straight and tall with their hands clasped behind their backs. They wore matching attire, satin overshirts with rank insignia stitched in. Black leggings tucked into boots.

These were uniforms.

The male spoke. "I am Eros," he said. "Welcome to my ship. This is Tanna, my second." She nodded her head, once.

"Thank you," said the colonel. "I am Thomas Edwards, and I hold rank with our military. This is Jonathon Harper, a policeman who enforces our laws. And this is Jeff Trent, a pilot trained to fly our aircraft."

"We are familiar with these roles," said Eros. Jeff felt uneasy with the way the alien spoke.

"Excuse me," he said, "but your words and what I'm hearing, they don't line up. Like there's a sync problem."

"You are correct," said Eros. "We are using a machine called the Dictial Robotery, and it is translating my words, and yours, as we voice them." He moved toward the panel with the language controls. "The speech is processed with -"

Harper didn't like Eros reaching for a switch. He drew his gun. "Now you two stay right where you're at," he said.

"Put your gun down," said Eros. "It is a coarse, ineffective weapon."

"Mister," said Jeff, drawing his pistol, "if you don't get away from that control board we'll show you just how effective they can be."

Tension rose in Eros. Tanna saw it. The pilot, the policeman, and her commander stood motionless, angry. Finally, Edwards took charge.

"Gentlemen, please, lower those guns. We're here to talk," he said.

With a nod, Jeff put his pistol away. It took Harper a few moments more to holster his gun. His eyes stayed locked on Eros. "All right," he said. "But you better move very carefully."

With confident steps, Edwards moved closer to the aliens. "Please, tell us why you've come to Earth."

Hope returned to Tanna as Eros spoke. "We are soldiers of our planet, but we did not come here as your enemies. We came only with friendly intentions. To talk. To ask your aid."

"Our aid?" said Edwards.

"Yes," said Eros. "Your aid for the whole universe. But your governments of Earth refused even to accept our existence. Even though you've seen us, heard our messages, you still refused to accept us."

"Why is it so important for you to contact the governments of Earth?" asked Edwards.

"Because of death. Because all you of Earth are idiots!"

That got Jeff's goat. "Now you just hold on, Buster," he said.

"No," said Eros. "*You* hold on. You are a headstrong young man."

"Take it easy, Jeff," said Harper.

Eros continued, pacing. "Your planet moved from swords to bullets too quickly. Then from bullets to grenades, killing more people. Then from grenades to bombs, destroying even larger areas and all the people in them. Your own people.

"When your scientists became involved, we'd hoped to see a more rationale approach to weapons development. Instead, they split the atom and created atomic bombs. Cities turned to dust. Entire populations eliminated. And now, you've gone beyond that, with your hydrogen bomb."

The colonel and Eros locked eyes. "Through all this, you still haven't evolved the wisdom to temper your remarkable destructive capabilities."

"It's true, we have a violent history," said Edwards. "But are you saying we're a threat to your planet? We can't even travel through space."

"You won't need to travel through space to destroy the universe. You are on the verge of creating a weapon to make that possible. The solaronite bomb."

"Solaronite?" said Edwards. "We have no such thing."

"You will. It is a by-product of nuclear fury, a new compound created in a fusion reaction. Your scientists will stumble upon solaronite soon enough. And as they have with every other new thing you've discovered, they will weaponize it. And given your history, you will not comprehend its strength, until it's too late."

Silence fell over the room. Tanna glanced at the engine controls and wished she'd set the launch to come sooner.

"The solaronite bomb is a way to explode particles of sunlight," said Eros.

"I wish I'd paid more attention in physics class," said Edwards. "Maybe it's the language computer, but I think you're talking about photons."

"Yes," said Eros. "Even now, your scientists are working on a way to harness the sun's rays, for energy. Limitless power from unseen particles, smaller than an atom. The solaronite will factor into this research soon after its discovery. And your inability to understand the consequences will result in the destruction of everything."

"Power you can't measure," said Jeff. "Fueled by particles you can't see. Triggered by a substance that can't be understood. Sounds like you come from a world without control."

Anger grew in Eros. They weren't listening. And this Earth person, Jeff Trent, shouldn't be here in the first place. The man held no importance. His home had the correct proximity to the cemetery for testing the decedents. The inhabitants were inconsequential.

An inconsequential man. Yet, he dared to speak for his planet.

"Sounds like if we develop this solaronite bomb," said Jeff, with a chuckle, "we'd be even a stronger nation than now."

"Stronger?" Rage took Eros. He stepped toward Jeff Trent. "You see? You see? Your stupid minds ... stupid! Stupid!!"

"That's all I'm taking from you!" said Jeff, and he took a swing at the alien, catching him on the chin. Tanna moved quickly between them as Harper and Edwards pulled Jeff away.

"Get back here!" said Harper.

"Let him finish," said Edwards.

Tanna spoke softly to Eros. "Time. Keep them talking, We just need a little more time."

"I am all right," said Eros, in a measured voice. He stepped away from Tanna and addressed the Earth men. "It's because of people like him all might be destroyed. Headstrong, violent! No use of the mind God gave you."

"You talk of God?" asked Jeff.

"You also think it impossible that we, too, might think of God? Yes, we've used drastic means, but you left us no alternative." Eros walked to a control panel and reached for a switch. "This is not a weapon, do not attack me. I am engaging our televisor so you may see outside."

The prime view showed Clay continuing his long trek to the saucer with Paula Trent unconscious in his arms. "She is unharmed, fainted," said Eros. "But if you make another violent move on my ship, I will have the dead one eliminate her."

"Paula," said Jeff. He swallowed his anger. He had to do as they said.

"My God. You monsters," said Harper. "That's Clay, Inspector Daniel Clay!" Everything he didn't want to face, didn't want to believe, displayed right there in front of him on the video screen.

"You demonstrate your ignorance Jonathon Harper," said Eros. "He ceased being that person the moment his brain stopped functioning. Now, he is simply dead flesh animated by our technology."

"He wasn't dead flesh until you murdered him," said Harper. "First you killed him, then you sick bastards dug him up and turned him into this ... this horror. You're making him attack people, hurt people. You're making him break the laws that, in life, he swore to uphold. Can't you see how foul, how mad this whole thing is?"

It became clear to Eros that this policeman, Harper, was a buffoon. An enforcer of primitive laws, created for primitive people. He'd never see the difference between the corpse and its former consciousness. He'd never understand the greater purpose Clay's death served.

The lieutenant stepped away from the screen and put a hand on Edwards shoulder. "Get what you need, Colonel Edwards. Get what you need and let's be done with all this." The colonel nodded and turned to Eros.

"Solaronite," he said. "I will take your message about solaronite to our leaders. Can you tell me more about it?"

"I will attempt to put this in terms you can understand. Take a can of your gasoline. Say this can of gasoline is the sun. Spread a thin a line of it to a ball, representing the Earth. Now, the gasoline represents the sunlight, the sun particles. Here we saturate the ball with the gasoline, the sunlight. Then we put a flame to the ball. The flame will speedily travel around the Earth, back along the line of gasoline to the can, or the sun itself. It will explode this source, and spread to every place that gasoline, our sunlight, touches. Explode the sunlight here, Gentlemen, and you explode the universe. Explode the sunlight here, and a chain reaction will occur, direct to the sun itself. And to all the planets that sunlight touches. To every planet in the universe. This is why you must stop. Failing that, we must stop you. Using all means at out disposal."

"He's mad," said Harper.

"Mad?" said Tanna. "Is it mad for you to destroy other people to save yourselves? You have done this. Is it mad for one country to destroy another to save themselves? You have also done this.

How then is it mad for one planet to destroy another who threatens all existence?"

No one from either planet had their eyes on the televisor screen 11. If they had, they would have seen an SFPD patrol car rolling in the front gate of Briar Glade Cemetery.

FOURTEEN

Just an Empty Void

Officer Larry Tucker pulled his patrol car next to Kelton's. He leapt out with his gun drawn. Paul Kelton paced around his vehicle, rubbing his neck. Tucker approached and saw both relief and confusion on the young officer's face.

"What happened?" asked Tucker. They were alone, so he holstered his gun.

"Are you the only one? I asked for lots of help!"

"You sounded drunk or something on the radio," said Tucker.

Kelton moved from confusion to fear. "It was horrible! He choked me until I passed out!"

"Look, what are you trying to say?" Tucker grabbed him by the shoulders. "Snap out of it. You're not making sense. Who choked you?"

"Inspector Clay."

"What?"

"It was Clay all right," said Kelton. "Still torn up, like when we found him. Well, his grave was busted into, right?"

"Are you telling me you saw a dead person walking in this graveyard?"

"Yes!" Kelton positioned himself in front of his car. "Clay came at me, right here. And I saw another, another … ghoul. A woman ghoul, just there, hunched by the window on the passenger side. And earlier, at the Trent's house, we fought another one, so that makes three. But that one turned into a skeleton on their patio."

Tucker pulled off his cap and scratched his head, trying to make sense of this. "I did hear the call about those remains at the Trent house."

"All of us saw it. The lieutenant, the colonel, everybody!"

"Where are they now?" asked Tucker, taking notice of the passenger door lying ten feet from the car.

"I don't know, but we've gotta find them," said Kelton. "Everyone except Mrs. Trent went off to look around. I stayed here to guard her. Then Clay showed up and put me out of the running. That was the second time a dead guy knocked me out tonight and I'm getting sick and tired of it!"

"You're off your rocker." Tucker shook his head. Kelton grabbed his arm.

"You gotta listen, Larry. When I came to, Mrs. Trent was gone. She's been taken, I tell you, and we've gotta find her."

Though he spoke nonsense, Kelton had real fear in his eyes. And with Mrs. Trent missing, Tucker had to act. "Okay," he said, "let's find the others. Show me which way they went."

* * *

With the automated launch imminent, Eros and Tanna both held hope. Their message had been heard. Soon, after a view from orbit, an Earth soldier with more perspective than anyone else on their planet would carry the message to his superiors.

Looking at the night sky through the observation dome, Eros spoke. "You understand, don't you Colonel Edwards, all of this can go away. In one big puff of smoke and ball of fire. Everything out there, the stars, the planets, all just an empty void."

"I believe you," said Edwards.

Tanna switched the vid-point nearest the ship onto the prime view. "Look," she said. "They've arrived."

The screen showed Clay, standing rigid, with Paula Trent still slung in his arms.

"Jeff, she's here," said Harper. "That thing is right outside with Paula."

"She'd better be all right," said Jeff.

"I assure you," said Eros. "She is unharmed."

* * *

The two officers had made their way to Inspector Clay's gravesite, hoping to find the others. When they got there, they saw the glow coming from the far side of the knoll.

They hurried toward it, but stopped short and ducked when they found the source of the light. "Holy cow!" said Tucker. "This is too much. A saucer, a real flying saucer!"

"And me without my camera," said Kelton. "Hey, look over there. Just like I told you, that's Inspector Clay."

"It's him, no doubt about it," said Tucker. "And he's got Mrs. Trent. Sorry Kelton, you were right all along."

"How do we stop him?"

"If we can get closer, maybe I can find an angle for a shot," said Tucker, drawing his gun.

"From all I've seen tonight guns won't do any good," said Kelton. "He's dead. I watched him get buried. How are we going to kill somebody that's already dead? Dead! And yet there he stands!"

"A couple of slugs might slow him down," said Tucker.

"No," said Kelton. "I emptied my revolver into the one on the patio and he never stopped coming."

Tucker put his weapon away. "I'm seeing it with my own eyes, that's the only reason I'm listening to you. There must be something we can do." He looked around and found a heavy branch about a yard long. "I bet you guys didn't try a club."

"You're right about that."

"Okay then," said Tucker. He gave the branch a few test swings. "I'll sneak up behind him and whop him over the head. If it doesn't knock him over, it may make him come after me. Either way, you grab Mrs. Trent and head in the opposite direction."

"You think it will work?"

"How should I know? Let's move."

As they got closer to their deceased commander, a whirring sound came from all around. "Crazy sort of buzzing," said Tucker. "You getting that?"

Yeah," said Kelton. "It happens when you get near one of those things. Puts you off-center. Try to ignore it."

They kept their steps quiet, but quick. Clay never turned toward them, never shifted at all. The officers shared a nod and a deep breath, then leapt forward. Tucker swung the branch with both hands. He struck the back of Clay's head so hard the branch broke in half. Clay didn't call out, gave no reaction at all. He simply fell to the ground and let go of Paula Trent.

Kelton got his arms around her and pulled her clear of her assailant. Tucker stood over Clay with the rest of the branch over his head, ready to strike again. But the former commander didn't move.

Tucker dropped the branch and joined Kelton. "Let's get her clear of the saucer," he said. "There might be Martians in there, or worse." They carried Paula Trent to the edge of the tree line, away from the ship.

* * *

Inside the saucer, the prime view carried this scene for all to see. "Your men have felled the big one," said Eros. "The blow must have jarred his receptor matrix. Tanna, use the reanimation console and connect the beam again."

"It will be done," said Tanna.

"Hold it, right there," said Harper. His revolver darted back and forth, from Eros to Tanna and back.

"Guns," said Eros. "Again, guns."

Harper kept his eyes on the aliens as he called over his shoulder. "Colonel Edwards," he said, "do you have everything you came here for?"

"Yes, yes I do," said Edwards.

"Good," said Harper. "because I'm taking these two in."

"What?" said Eros.

"Lieutenant Harper, think about what you're doing," said Edwards.

"Oh, I have. They're responsible for at least three murders. And Heaven knows what other crimes against nature. No, I won't let them get away with it. I'm bringing them in."

With a sharp hum, the navigation panel lit up. The engines started. Sixty millicycles had passed. The timed launch sequence had begun.

"What's that?" asked Edwards.

Jeff Trent approached the navigation panel. "This board just went live." He toggled a few of the switches. "I can't make out the symbols, but that rumble sure sounds like the engines."

"Stop pawing at that," said Eros. "You might endanger all of us." He took a step toward Trent, then found Harper's revolver in his face.

"You're already 'endangered,'" said Harper. "Now tell Mr. Trent how this panel works." He was so focused on getting Eros to talk, he didn't see Tanna moving in.

"Harper, look out," said Edwards. Too late. Tanna grabbed Harper's wrist and pulled the gun away from Eros.

Eros lunged to the navigation panel and shoved Jeff Trent away. "These engines are precision machines. You can't just slap at the controls," he said.

Then Jeff hit Eros. Hard. It brought the alien's rage out front. He hit back. The two of them thrashed around the deck, falling against control stations, sending random commands to systems all over the saucer.

Tanna struggled with Harper, trying to wrestle the gun away from him. It fired twice as they grappled. One bullet pierced the landing circuits panel, sending it into darkness. The second punched a hole in the thrust constraints. Smoke, then sparks burst from the rupture.

More sparks and smoke belched from the field generator board after Eros bounced Jeff against it.

"Damn it, Harper, the ship's going haywire," said Edwards. "Let the woman go and help me find the hatch." The colonel tracked along the wall, examining buttons and levers.

Harper and Tanna held for a moment, staring hatred at one another. Then the lieutenant pushed her away and ran to the place where they came in. "Pretty sure this was the spot, Colonel," he said. There were too many dials and switches. "But I can't tell one of these gadgets from another."

Tanna leapt to the navigation panel to evaluate the damage. She found the controls unresponsive, dark. Worse yet, their landing cylinder refused to retract. When the gravity aversion engines reached full power, the extended cylinder would have a disastrous effect on the saucer's profile.

The ship would tear itself apart. "Eros," she called. "Eros! We've got to stop the launch!"

* * *

Outside, Paula Trent regained consciousness. Kelton rubbed her hands. "Mrs. Trent?" he said. "Mrs. Trent, can you hear me? Are you all right?"

"Oh, I think so. Where's the car?" She looked up at the saucer. "My God, they're here!"

"Maybe we should move further back," said Tucker. "That ship is making some ugly noises."

"Where's Jeff?" asked Paula. "Where are the others?"

Kelton and Tucker shared a look. "Hey," said Kelton, "do you think they might be inside?"

* * *

A slender lever on the wall sat in an oval recess. Edwards pulled it, and the hatch appeared just as it had before. "Got it!" Harper moved through the opening and the colonel called back to Jeff. "Get out of there now, Jeff!"

Jeff heard him. His eyes burned from the smoke. He had a hard time breathing, too. With both hands, he pushed Eros away with everything he had, then he did a blind run out the hatch.

The three men gathered in the elevator. Edwards spotted another control lever and pulled it. The hatch vanished and the elevator dropped.

The doorway levers were recessed and hard to see, but now that he knew what they looked like, the colonel had little trouble finding them.

The men made it to the long, curved hallway, then tumbled out into the cool air of Earth.

There, Harper joined his officers. Jeff held his wife. Edwards kept looking at the saucer, hoping to see Eros and Tanna run out.

* * *

Eros had lost consciousness. When Trent shoved him, his head struck the televisor unit leaving a deep gash on his temple.

"Eros!" called Tanna, "Eros, wake up! The landing cylinder won't retract. We're in danger!"

The ship rose. Outside, the force of the engines pushed the Earth people down once again. This time, the ship's ascent had an awkward wobble. With the base extended, it lost its saucer shape.

Eros remained motionless. After several attempts at repair, Tanna rose from the navigation controls. She had run out of options. The ship would shatter before they reached the stratosphere and there was nothing she could do to stop it.

At the comm station, she prepared a beacon. It had a karradium housing, designed to survive the ship's destruction. Its propulsion system would carry her final message home.

She wanted this last communication to bring hope from their dealings with Earth. Her report said the Earth people had heard and understood all Eros had told them. The warnings about solaronite would reach the planet's leaders. Unfortunately, their ship suffered a catastrophic malfunction on launch. They were lost, but their Earth mission, the last mission for Commander Eros, was a success.

Tanna looked through the observation dome and watched the beacon sail away. She wished for one more look at Jupiter, but it wasn't meant to be. The Moon would have to do.

* * *

The saucer continued its lopsided ascent, increasing its speed, occasionally venting flames. "They're in trouble," said Jeff, holding Paula close.

In a few moments, the ship had gained so much altitude everyone lost sight of it. "You think they got away?" asked Harper.

"Maybe," said the colonel. "If they got that fire out, just maybe."

Without warning, a brilliant flash filled the nighttime sky. Everyone shielded their eyes from the searing light as a low rumble, like distant thunder, rose in the air.

Then, as quickly as they had materialized, the light and sound faded. The moonlit night over San Fernando was peaceful once more.

Jeff opened his eyes to find Paula looking at him. "It's over," she whispered. They shared a smile.

A sense of satisfaction swept over Harper. "That's the last we'll see of them," he said.

"It's certainly the end of Eros and Tanna," said Edwards. "But there are others."

Kelton stood over the body of Inspector Clay. "Look, he's just like the other one," he said. As with the old man, only bones remained.

It gave Paula a start. "Hey," she said, "did you find that woman, that thing yet?"

"She's right," said Kelton. "There's another ghoul running loose."

"If there's any more of them, they'll look like him," said Edwards. "With the ship gone, they have no control. It's uncanny what they can do. They're so far ahead of us."

"What's next, Colonel Edwards?" asked Harper.

"I'm going to do exactly what I told them," said Edwards "I'll take their message, their warning about solaronite to Washington. From there, it will be heard by leaders all around the world."

"You think they'll listen?" asked Jeff.

"Based on what I've seen," said the colonel, "they don't have any other choice."

Epilogue

A LAKE OF JADE

Weeks later, in Jornada del Muerto, New Mexico, an army team gathered glass from the desert sand. Major Scott Guy was in charge. The unit had a small command center set up under a canopy; nothing more than a few folding tables and chairs along with a station for food and drinks. Two square miles of wasteland had been fenced off and divided into dig sites. Down a makeshift road, a series of tents served as housing.

Under the canopy, Guy read from a flash folder, reviewing his orders for the rest of the week. He pulled the string and destroyed it as a jeep hauling a sealed crate pulled in from dig site 112. Some of the men transferred the crate to a panel truck, loaded with more crates just like it. The jeep's driver, Private Walters, got some water and joined the major.

They traded salutes. "Another full box, Sir," said Walters. "And they started another one before we pulled away."

"Orders are clear, Private," said Guy. "We're going to keep sweeping and packing the stuff up until there isn't any left. We may be here a long time."

"Boy, that's the truth. We're finding more of the red glass than the green in this area. Don't know if it matters."

"Have a seat, Private," said Guy, kicking a chair out from the table. "It's going to take them a while to log everything."

Walters refilled his water then plopped in the chair. "Don't mind if I do, Sir."

"You know, we aren't the first crew out here," said Guy. "They thought they got it all three years ago. Bulldozed the whole area. Stored all they found at the dump site east of Holloman."

"I don't think that crew was very careful. We're filling a lot of crates, and we aren't even looking hard." The private handed Major Guy a copy of the *Silver City Daily Press*. "Hey, did you see this?"

The paper was folded to the Amazing Criswell's syndicated column. The headline read OUR SECRET WAR WITH FLYING SAUCERS!

The column told of an alien ship landing in a San Fernando, California cemetery. Experiments with the dead. Intervention by the police and the military.

> My friend, you have read these facts, based on sworn testimony. Can you prove that it didn't happen? Perhaps on your way home, someone will pass you in the dark, and you will never know it, for they will be from outer space. Many scientists believe that another world is watching us at this moment. We once laughed at the horseless carriage, the airplane, the telephone, the electric light, vitamins, radio, and even television! And now some of us laugh at outer space. God help us - in the future.

"What do you think of that?" said Walters. "Right there in the paper for everyone to read."

The major tossed the paper on the table and shook his head. "Good thing nobody takes this creep for real. Last week he said Mae West will become President of the United States, and then the two of them are going to travel to the moon."

Private Walters' brow became deeply furrowed. "Criswell said that?" he asked.

"Yeah, he did." The major got himself a coffee. "And the igno-ramus is still getting published."

Another jeep pulled in with another crate.

"This trintle-glass must be pretty special," said Walters.

"It's called *trinitite*. And you can't find it anywhere else."

"Why not?"

The major looked out on the desert. "Back in 1945," he said, "when they tested the atom bomb out here, the energies were so intense that the sand, the support gantry, the electric wires, and anything else in the central blast zone all got fused. Everything superheated, stirred around in a nuclear whirlwind, and became something new. When it was all over, the desert floor looked like a lake of jade."

"And they called it trinitite," said Walters.

"And that's what we're after. Such a fuss." Guy clasped his hands together and reached up high, stretching his back. "You know, back in the day any schmoe could come out here and grab all the trinitite they wanted. They made jewelry out of it. Keychains, paperweights. Tourist trap stuff. Then the government got worried the material might have some kind of hidden radiation."

Walters bristled. "Radiation? We've been wading in the stuff."

"Relax, Private," said Guy. "They had it wrong. You've seen the Geiger readings; the glass is fine. But at the time, fear drove the decision making, so the brass closed the place off. Shut the whole area down."

The men watched a truck with five soldiers and racks of equipment roll out toward the dig site. "Well," said Walters, "we're sure open for business now."

"Ain't that the truth," said Guy. "Don't understand why there's all this sudden interest, though. Something to do with the way the stuff reacts to light."

The following pages feature promotional material from the original theatrical run of *Plan 9 From Outer Space* as well as images from the film. Used by permission.

UNSPEAKABLE HORRORS FROM OUTER SPACE PARALYZE THE LIVING AND RESURRECT THE DEAD!
PLAN 9 FROM OUTER SPACE
with
BELA LUGOSI
VAMPIRA
LYLE TALBOT
A J. Edward Reynolds Production
Produced and Directed by
Edward D. Wood, Jr.
a DCA release
THEATRE

SYNOPSIS

Reports of flying saucers and mysterious deaths terrify the residents of San Fernando Valley. Although the Army has had open combat with the space ships, the government publicly denies their existence to avoid international panic.

In outer space, The Ruler (John Breckenridge) sends Eros (Dudley Manlove) and Tanna (Joanna Lee) to destroy the earth before the earth destroys the universe with nuclear testing. They institute Plan 9, which is the resurrection of the earth dead. In a San Fernando cemetery, they start with two corpses (Vampira and Bela Lugosi) who subsequently kill two gravediggers. Inspector Clay (Tor Johnson), a giant of a man goes to the cemetery to investigate the double murder and is killed by the ghouls.

At the edge of the cemetery is the home of Jeff and Paula Trent (Gregory Walcott and Mona McKinnon). Jeff, an airline pilot, having seen the saucers, is naturally disturbed when he has to leave Paula. After he has gone, the ghoul man breaks in and attacks Paula. She escapes through the cemetery to the highway and is rescued by a passing motorist. As part of Plan 9, the newly-buried Inspector Clay is resurrected and joins the two other ghouls.

At the Pentagon, General Roberts (Lyle Talbot) sends Col. Edwards (Tom Keene), who has seen previous combat with the saucers, to San Fernando Valley to investigate.

Meanwhile Eros and Tanna take off for outer space to show their ghouls to The Ruler. He decides that they are to destroy one ghoul and complete their assignment to destroy the earth.

The ship returns to the cemetery and the doomed ghoul appears at the Trent home where Police Lt. Harper (Duke Moore) and Col. Edwards are questioning Paula. Their attempts to shoot the ghoul are futile but suddenly a ray from the space ship turns the ghoul into a skeleton.

The men proceed to search the cemetery and succeed in finding the ship. Paula, who has been left behind, is captured by the late Inspector Clay and is being carried towards the space ship but is rescued when some policemen overpower the ghoul.

Jeff, Col. Edwards and Lt. Harper enter the space ship and Jeff attacks Eros. During the struggle, several delicate instruments are smashed and flying sparks cause a fire. Tanna rushes to get the ship into flight but Jeff, Col. Edwards and Lt. Harper escape just before it takes off. On the ground, they watch the spectacular explosion of the flaming ship in mid-air.

"PLAN 9 FROM OUTER SPACE" Chilling Combination of SCIENCE FICTION — ACTION — HORROR

"Plan 9 From Outer Space" now playing at the . . . . Theatre, is a chilling combination of science fiction — action — horror.

Packed with thrills, it shows furious combat between our army and the saucer men; invincible ghouls brought to life by the spacemen; blood-thirsty ghouls attacking American citizens; the spectacular explosion of the flaming space ship.

"Plan 9 From Outer Space" is a J. Edward Reynolds Production, written and directed by Edward D. Wood, Jr. and starring Vampira, Tor Johnson, Tom Keene, Lyle Talbot and the late, great horror-man Bela Lugosi. Filmed on location, it is a violent film as timely as today's newspaper headlines.

Invaders from outer space turn Vampira into a blood-thirsty ghoul in "Plan 9 From Outer Space" now playing at   Theatre.

Scene 1A

"PLAN 9 FROM OUTER S.. ACE" NOW AT ....THEATRE MARKS BELA LUGOSI'S FINAL APPEARANCE

The most famous horror-man of all time, the late Bela Lugosi, can be seen in his final film, "Plan 9 From Outer Space" which is now playing at the ....Theatre.

Mr. Lugosi's long and successful career came to an end shortly after the completion of "Plan 9" which was his third collaboration with his long-time friend, writer-director Edward D. Wood, Jr. (the others: "Bride of the Monster" and "I Led Two Lives").

The veteran actor earned his place in Hollywood's Horror Hall of Fame for his unforgettable performance as Dracula.

In "Plan 9," which is a J. Edward Reynolds Production also starring Tor Johnson, Vampira, Lyle Talbot and other top stars, Mr. Lugosi portrays a bloodthirsty ghoul ressurected by invaders from outer space.

A Ghoul (Tor Johnson) resurrected by invaders from outer space abducts beautiful Paula Trent (Mona McKinnon) in a scene from "Plan 9 From Outer Space"
Scene 2A

2 col. x 55 lines — (110 lines)

2 col. x 33 lines — (66 lines)

The following ACCESSORIES are available from National Screen Service
1 SHEET · 11 x 14's
(Set of 8)
8 x 10 STILLS · TRAILER

Special
Ad
Mat
No. 1
only
35¢

1 col. x 87 lines

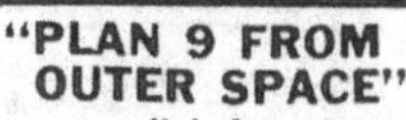

1 col. x 16 lines

a *DCA* release

DISTRIBUTORS CORPORATION OF AMERICA, 1560 BROADWAY, NEW YORK 36, N.Y. · JUdson 6-7800

WARNER
STANLEY WARNER THEATRE

NEW DOUBLE FEATURE
Beautiful and Proud...
"LIANE,
JUNGLE GODDESS"
in EASTMAN COLOR
FEATURE NO. 2
"PLAN 9 FROM
OUTER SPACE"
with Bela Lugosi

Kiddy MATINEE

WARNER
Saturday

4 HOUR SHOW
DOORS OPEN 11 30 A.M.
CARTOONS plus
"PLAN 9 FROM
OUTER SPACE"
Plus FREE
TRICKS or TREAT BAGS
Adults, 65c   Children, 25c

"You are interested in the unknown, the mysterious, the unexplainable. That is why you are here." (Ch. 1)

"The old man standing next to the pastor wasn't paying him any mind.
He focused on the casket, resting below." (Ch. 1)

"Their aircraft settled. The light subsided revealing a flying saucer
hovering in front of the plane." (Ch. 2)

"We are requesting landing instructions.
And we have something to report." (Ch. 2)

"Ahead of them, somehow, the gaunt woman
waited with her claw-like fingers reaching." (Ch. 2)

"He saw her everywhere. Every bit of this house manifested something about her." (Ch. 2)

"The accompanying article said a carload of people witnessed a saucer flying near the 101 Freeway." (Ch. 5)

"Behind the same knoll at the Briar Glade Cemetery where it landed a week before, the saucer settled in." (Ch. 4)

"A great object flew overhead and, for just a few seconds, lit the area like a baseball stadium." (Ch. 4)

"Plan 9 is the most viable. Death is universally feared
and misunderstood on this planet." (Ch. 6)

"The dead responded well to the commands, and the
beam controlling them had considerable range." (Ch. 7)

"And inch by inch, the corpse of Daniel Clay struggled out of the ground." (Ch. 7)

"The deceased pair came into the room with Tanna" (Ch. 8)

"Shocking facts ... about grave robbers from outer space." (Ch. 11)

"Paula Trent was surrounded by the dead." (Ch. 12)

"They're responsible for at least three murders ...
I'm bringing them in." (Ch. 14)

About the Author

When Bret Nelson isn't writing stories, he's making TV shows and games. He's worked with Kermit the Frog, Buzz Lightyear, and Conan the Cimmerian. Right now, he's working on things he can't talk about (that's what the contracts say).

9 781960 721631